P9-CAN-102

THE HAIRY BEAST

IN THE

WOODS

OTHER YEARLING BOOKS YOU WILL ENJOY:

THE HAUNTING OF HILLCREST, *Mary Anderson*
THE LEIPZIG VAMPIRE, *Mary Anderson*
TERROR UNDER THE TENT, *Mary Anderson*
THE THREE SPIRITS OF VANDERMEER MANOR,
Mary Anderson
PRISONER OF VAMPIRES, *Nancy Garden*
THE HEADLESS CUPID, *Zilpha Keatley Snyder*
THE WITCHES OF WORM, *Zilpha Keatley Snyder*
THE EGYPT GAME, *Zilpha Keatley Snyder*
THE VELVET ROOM, *Zilpha Keatley Snyder*
BLACK AND BLUE MAGIC, *Zilpha Keatley Snyder*

YEARLING BOOKS/YOUNG YEARLINGS/YEARLING CLASSICS
are designed especially to entertain and enlighten
young people. Patricia Reilly Giff, consultant to this
series, received her bachelor's degree from Mary-
mount College. She holds a master's degree in history
from St. John's University, and a Professional Diploma
in Reading from Hofstra University. She was a teacher
and reading consultant for many years, and is the
author of numerous books for young readers.

For a complete listing of all Yearling titles, write to
Dell Readers Service, P. O. Box 1045,
South Holland, IL 60473.

MOSTLY MONSTERS

THE HAIRY BEAST
IN THE
WOODS

Mary Anderson

A YEARLING BOOK

Published by
Dell Publishing
a division of
Bantam Doubleday Dell Publishing Group, Inc.
666 Fifth Avenue
New York, New York 10103

Copyright © 1989 by Mary Anderson

All rights reserved. No part of this book may be reproduced
or transmitted in any form or by any means, electronic or
mechanical, including photocopying, recording, or by any
information storage and retrieval system, without the written
permission of the Publisher, except where permitted by law.

The trademark Yearling® is registered in the U.S. Patent and
Trademark Office.

ISBN: 0-440-40178-X

Printed in the United States of America

May 1989

10 9 8 7 6 5 4 3

CW

Chapter One

"I DESPISE WAITING," CASSIE GRUMBLED AS SHE SAT IN THE entrance hall of Ludlington Manor. "I've already been waiting for absolute ages!"

"That's a big lie," said Barney, who was seated next to her.

Cassie gave him a haughty look. "*Excusez-moi*? I don't know you, nor do I care to, so what's it your business?"

"*I* was here first," Barney explained. "I'm waiting, too. In fact," he added grandly, "I spent the whole day on the bus just to get here."

Cassie laughed sarcastically. "Well, I've just flown all the way from Zurich. That's in Switzerland, you know."

"I know where it is," Barney snapped. "So what?"

"So naturally I can't be kept waiting," Cassie continued. "It's disgustingly rude when you consider I've come so far to meet my great-aunt Alexandra."

1

Barney looked at her in disbelief. *"Your* great-aunt? Impossible. I'm here to meet *my* great-aunt Alexandra." He thought a moment. "You don't suppose—I mean—do you think the two of us could be related?"

Cassie inched away. "What a depressing thought, but I suppose anything's possible. What's your name?"

"Barney Prescott. What's yours?"

"Cassie Hastings, of the New York Hastings, naturally."

"No kidding? I never heard of you."

Cassie inched farther away. "I certainly never heard of you, either. Yet I suppose we could be second cousins or something. I've tons of those I've never met. They're from another branch of the family—all poor relations."

Barney threw Cassie a filthy look. "Know something? I think *you're* disgustingly rude."

Cassie shrugged and turned away. "Who cares?"

Staring at one another, they each grew silent. Presently Cassie crossed her legs, then brushed her long blond hair behind her ear in an affected gesture. "She can't possibly be *your* great-aunt," she protested.

Barney nervously adjusted his eyeglasses. "Who says? She's my great-aunt Alexandra. I've come here to live with her for a whole year. My parents said it's all arranged."

Cassie seemed shocked. *"Au contraire,* I'm sure there's been some horrid mistake. *I've* been sent here to live with great-aunt Alexandra."

"Maybe she wants both of us to stay with her."

"Both of us? Ridiculous!"

Barney agreed. "You're right, that's a stinking idea."

Beyond the entrance hall, out of Cassie and Barney's sight, the library doors slowly inched open. From inside, Alexandra Ludlington was secretly observing the first meeting between her grandniece and grandnephew. As she peeked through the door she smiled. "Yes, it's going splendidly," she said. "The children are getting to know each other. In a few minutes, they'll be the best of friends."

Oliver Crenshaw, her longtime friend and business manager, sat in a leather chair, looking extremely agitated. "Alex," he scolded, "stop snooping by that door. A woman of your age should have more decorum."

"Nonsense," she replied, continuing to observe the children. "A woman of my age should enjoy herself, which is precisely what I always do. So far, my plan is working wonderfully. You know, Ollie, this may turn out to be one of my very best plans."

Oliver Crenshaw had lived through many such "plans." "It's your *worst*," argued Crenshaw. "It's ludicrous. I've known you for years and you've never initiated a more mindless idea. Alex, I beg you, don't do this! Face it, you can't take two children who've never met and throw them together indiscriminately."

Alexandra Ludlington looked offended. "Indiscriminate? Nonsense, Ollie. I've carefully selected these two children. I've spent weeks on researching them. I've compiled mountains of information on them both."

Oliver Crenshaw tucked his finely manicured hands

3

into the pockets of his expensively tailored suit, then began pacing the library. "Yes, I've read through those files, Alex. That's why I'm worried."

"But why?" she asked. "According to all our information Barney Prescott is a dear little boy."

"Okay, I agree the nine-year-old boy seems all right," Crenshaw conceded, "despite the fact he's from a poor background. But the *girl*. According to your reports the girl appears to be incorrigible: an overindulged delinquent, past the point of rehabilitation."

Alexandra Ludlington brushed a wisp of silver-gray hair away from her forehead, then chuckled. "She's only eleven, Ollie. She's hardly a candidate for capital punishment!"

Crenshaw grabbed Cassie's file from the library desk. "Oh, no? Listen to this. Her parents provide her with an exorbitant monthly allowance, which she squanders. She's either been thrown out of or run away from every decent boarding school in Europe. Good heavens, Alex, she actually tried to burn one school down!"

Alexandra Ludlington grabbed the file and threw it onto the desk. "Merely hearsay evidence. If Cassie *has* done incorrigible things, I'm sure it's because she needs *attention*."

"Or *incarceration*," Crenshaw argued. "You must stop trying to rehabilitate the world, Alex. Not even *you* are rich enough to do that. It's best you leave things as they are."

"You're not backing out on our bargain, are you, Ollie?" she asked suspiciously. "After all, it's only for one year."

4

Crenshaw sighed. "My word is my bond, Alex, you know that. I promised I'd tutor these two children for one year."

"And be our traveling companion, too," she added. "Don't forget."

"I've always been loyal to the Ludlington family," said Crenshaw dutifully. "I've handled things ever since your husband died and I'll continue to do so. But I feel obliged to inform you, I think this is a reckless, ill-fated, badly conceived idea."

Alexandra Ludlington smiled and patted Crenshaw on the back. "Well, I don't."

"But we know absolutely *nothing* about children, Alex," he protested.

"Then it's time we started learning. Won't it be fun? Come along, let's meet my niece and nephew now."

Chapter Two

THE HOUSEKEEPER LED BARNEY AND CASSIE DOWN THE marble hall of Ludlington Manor. Barney's heart pounded with anticipation. Nervously he readjusted his glasses. Barney's parents had told him he would have a year of fun and adventure. But they'd never mentioned he'd have to spend it with a snooty, sour-faced, spoiled-rotten *girl*. Despite this he vowed to make the best of things.

Cassie, on the other hand, had no such intention. If she didn't like it at Ludlington Manor, she'd run away—and that was that.

The housekeeper pushed open the large oak doors of the library. "Come in, children," said Alexandra Ludlington, smiling. "Ollie and I have been waiting to meet you."

Oliver Crenshaw peeked out from behind the door. "Don't have them call me *that*," he insisted. "Make them call me Crenshaw. I must remain an *authority* figure."

"Oh. All right, Ollie," said Alexandra Ludlington. She drew the children nearer. "Cassie, Barney, let me introduce Crenshaw. He'll be your tutor for the year. As for me, I'm less formal, so call me Aunt Alex. The four of us should get along splendidly, don't you agree?"

Barney stared at the imposing, well-dressed man. "Our *tutor*? I've never had such a fancy teacher before."

"Crenshaw isn't really a teacher," Aunt Alex explained, "even though he's considered the world's smartest man. Well, at least he *was* considered that until last year. Ollie was listed in the *Guinness Book of Records*."

"Really?" asked Barney.

"That's right, young man," said Crenshaw proudly. "Up until last year."

"What happened last year?"

"A man in Philadelphia scored one point higher on the IQ test," he explained angrily, "but I bear him no ill will."

"You don't look very smart to me," Cassie observed.

"But he is," said Aunt Alex. "Ask Crenshaw anything and he'll know the answer. That's why he's been my business manager all these years. I knew it would take the world's smartest man to manage the estate of one of the country's richest women."

"Are you really *that* rich?" asked Barney.

"So they tell me. Rich enough, at any rate."

Cassie wasn't impressed. "I didn't expect to have a

7

tutor while I was here. I thought this was a social visit."

Crenshaw sneered. "From what I've heard, you're not a very social person."

Cassie grew defensive. "What's that mean?"

"It means Alexandra Ludlington isn't a woman to be taken advantage of," he warned. "For the next year, you two will have certain privileges, but you'll also have to be on good behavior."

"I'm always well behaved," said Barney. "My mom says so."

"I'll bet you are," said Aunt Alex. "My research files corroborate that."

Cassie was getting suspicious. "Files? Have you been checking up on us?"

Crenshaw walked toward the desk, picked up Cassie's file, and waved it above his head threateningly. "Of course. How else could your great-aunt pick her two neediest relatives?"

Cassie was furious. "How dare you? I'm not needy. My parents are very wealthy people."

"I'm not needy, either," Barney protested. "My folks aren't rich, but I'm not needy."

"Of course you're not," said Aunt Alex. She glared at Crenshaw. "What an unfortunate choice of words, Ollie."

"But, Alex, you said . . ."

"I said we'd all get along splendidly," she scolded, "so don't start trouble. Naturally I took *time* selecting the children. That's important, since we'll all be traveling together."

"I can't wait," said Barney eagerly. "Where will we go?"

"Wherever the winds take us," she replied. "Your respective parents agree the year will prove most rewarding."

"But *where* will the winds take us?" Barney persisted.

"I'm not sure," Aunt Alex admitted. "They might take us to Maine; I've a charming cottage there by the sea. Or we could go to Austria, where I have a lovely chalet in the mountains. Or perhaps we'll go visiting instead. I love visiting old friends. I have a dear old friend in Minnesota whom I haven't seen in ages; maybe we'll go there. What do you think, Barney? Would you like to go to any of those places?"

"Sure, I'd like to go to all of them."

"I wouldn't," said Cassie, "particularly not Minnesota."

Barney threw her a filthy look. "I'd especially love to go to Minnesota, Aunt Alex."

"So would I," said Aunt Alex with delight. "I have a real craving to see my old friend Winnie Comstock. Seven years ago she moved out into the woods of Blue Ridge and I haven't seen her since. I imagine it's quite rustic and beautiful out there—a perfect place to visit."

"Not so fast," said Crenshaw. "No one is going anywhere until we're all properly acquainted."

Aunt Alex agreed. "You begin, Barney. Tell us something about yourself."

"I have three brothers, two dogs, and four cats," he explained.

Aunt Alex smiled. "What a charming family. How about you, Cassie?"

"I have no brothers, no sisters, and I hate pets," she said sullenly. Then she stared at the file on Aunt Alex's desk. "But I'll bet you know that already. Why have you asked us here? I don't need your charity."

"I'm not offering charity, child," Aunt Alex explained. "I'm offering experience, adventure, and companionship."

"I don't need that, either," she protested.

"Perhaps *I* need the companionship, Cassie. Old people get lonely, too, you know. Even rich old people. When I devised this plan I thought it would be an ideal arrangement for all of us. Barney would get to travel, which I know he's always wanted to do, and you'd have some stability in your life."

Cassie wasn't listening. She was still staring at the file resting on the desk, determined to steal it. *No one* had a right to spy into her private life.

Cassie slowly approached the desk. When she thought no one was looking, she slipped the file behind her back, then tucked it into her bag. What did it reveal? she wondered. Did it list *every* terrible thing she'd ever done? What an awful thought!

"I won't keep either of you against your will," Aunt Alex continued. "If you prefer to leave . . ."

"Not me," said Barney. "Let's start our year of fun and adventure."

Cassie was uncertain. "Will my parents still send me my monthly allowance?"

"Certainly," said Aunt Alex. "That's all been arranged."

Cassie thought of Mme. Fresnay, headmistress of The Academy for Young Ladies in Zurich. Compared with that spiteful old poker face, Aunt Alex didn't seem so bad. "All right, I'll stay."

Aunt Alex was delighted. "A wise decision, you won't regret it. Wonderful, things are all settled." She paced back and forth excitedly. "What shall I do first? I'll call Winnie, naturally. But I won't tell her I'm bringing the children; that will be my surprise."

"Do you think that's wise?" asked Crenshaw. "Personally, I wouldn't care for such a *startling* surprise."

"Winnie *loves* children," Aunt Alex explained. "She'll be thrilled. Since we're going up north, Cassie and Barney will need proper clothing. We'll buy them both new outfits."

At the mention of clothes, Cassie perked up. "Will I get an entire new wardrobe?"

"Certainly," said Aunt Alex. "We'll have everything delivered: long johns, woolen mufflers, earmuffs, rubber boots—and hot-water bottles, of course."

Cassie frowned. "I mean high-fashion items."

Aunt Alex laughed. "Bless you, child, you won't need to be fashionable in the woods, just warm and cozy."

Barney was excited. "Good, we're going to Minnesota right away."

Aunt Alex was equally excited. "The morning can't come soon enough. My housekeeper, Nora, will show you children to your rooms while Crenshaw and I make the arrangements. We'll see you both at dinner."

Cassie glanced over at Oliver Crenshaw. "Does *he* have to come along with us?"

Crenshaw gave Cassie a strained smile through tightly clenched teeth. "I certainly do, young lady. You shouldn't grow up to be both ignorant *and* rude."

Barney giggled as Nora ushered them from the library. As they hurried down the marble entrance hall he poked Cassie. "Crenshaw sure told you off."

Cassie poked him back. "Don't speak to me, you little creep."

"C'mon, let's be friends. After all, we're spending a whole year together."

"I never said I'd stay for a year. And I never said I'd be your friend."

"Who cares? I don't want to be your friend, anyway. I only offered because of Aunt Alex."

"Aren't you the goody-goody!"

"Who wants to be friends with a *thief?* I saw you steal those papers off Aunt Alex's desk and I'm *telling*." Defiantly, Barney headed back toward the library.

Cassie grabbed his arm. "Don't tell anyone about that. If you do, I'll . . ."

"You'll what?" asked Barney mockingly.

"I'll—I'll *poison* you," threatened Cassie.

"Quit kidding."

"Who says I'm kidding?"

Nora noticed the children had stopped midway down the hall. "Come along, children, your rooms are waiting." She started up the stairs.

Cassie held tight to Barney's arm.

"Let go," he pleaded. "What's in those papers, any-how? Why'd you steal them?"

"It's a list of all the awful things I've ever done," she admitted. "And it's none of Aunt Alex's business. It's none of yours, either. Don't you dare tell I stole them."

Barney was getting worried. "Awful things? Have you really done awful things?"

Cassie was pleasantly surprised by Barney's gullibility.

"Terrible, disgusting things," she said dramatically. "And I know lots about poison, too. Rat poison is my specialty. In a big old house like this I'll bet there are lots of rats skittering around the basement. And lots of rat poison hidden in the kitchen." She began twisting Barney's arm. "Say anything to Aunt Alex and you might find some hidden in your dinner."

Nora leaned over the banister. "Hurry up, what's keeping you?"

Barney loosened himself from Cassie's grip. "I'm coming," he shouted, running toward the stairs.

Barney could hardly wait to get into his room and slam the door behind him!

That night, Barney poked at his dinner. The soup didn't kill him, so he decided it was safe to eat the chicken—very *carefully*.

"You eat like a little bird," observed Aunt Alex. "Why pick at your food like that, Barney? A growing boy should have a much bigger appetite."

"I want to *continue* growing," he mumbled.

Cassie was delighted. Her threat had really frightened Barney. It might be fun teasing him for an entire *year*.

The maid placed the chocolate mousse dessert on the table. Cassie looked at it admiringly. "I once watched a famous French chef prepare this," she explained teasingly. "He told me chocolate mousse is so rich, it can disguise any taste—even the taste of *poison*."

Crenshaw took a bite. "What a somber thought."

Although Barney adored chocolate, he pushed his aside.

"By the way," said Aunt Alex, "I've misplaced Cassie's file. Have either of you children seen it?"

"I haven't seen anything," said Barney nervously.

"It doesn't really matter," said Aunt Alex. "That file represents the past, and we're only interested in the future. And for the next year we'll make that future *together*."

Oliver Crenshaw groaned audibly.

Gloating, Cassie stuck her tongue out at Barney.

Barney continued to stare at his uneaten chocolate mousse.

Chapter Three

"CASSIE, PAY ATTENTION TO YOUR GEOGRAPHY LESSON," Crenshaw insisted.

Cassie slumped in the airline seat and stared out the window of the plane. "It's bad enough I have to go to Minnesota, do I have to *learn* about it, too?"

"Certainly," he replied. "Flying time should never be wasted. When we land, you should have all these facts committed to memory."

"I'm not interested in facts about Minnesota," she argued. "Who cares about the altitude and population?"

Crenshaw put the book down. "It's clear you have no talent for academics. Tutoring you will be a difficult job."

"I remember everything you taught us," said Barney smugly. "The state tree of Minnesota is the red pine, and the state bird is the loon."

15

"Who cares?" said Cassie. "I might turn into a loony myself, stuck out here in the boonies."

"Don't worry," said Aunt Alex sympathetically. "If geography isn't your strongpoint, perhaps it's poetry. You just concocted a little rhyme." She leaned back in her seat and sighed. "My friend Winnie was always writing poetry. We'd often have great times together in the old days. We'd play chess and I'd listen to Winnie read her poems. I've really missed her."

"Why did she move so far away?" asked Barney.

"I don't know," Aunt Alex admitted. "One day Winnie suddenly packed up and moved into the woods. She said she couldn't live near people any longer."

"She sounds *mysterious*," said Barney.

"She sounds *weird*," said Cassie.

"No, she's great fun," said Aunt Alex. "You'll love Winnie. *Everyone* loves Winnie Comstock."

"I was wrong," said Cassie, glancing around the town of Blue Ridge as the bus drove off into the distance. "This is worse than the boonies, it's the end of the world! What a dumpy place."

Aunt Alex glanced around the barren town. The road looked deserted, and no one was strolling the streets. "I'll admit it took us forever to get here, but at least the journey is almost over."

It had taken an entire day of traveling to arrive in Blue Ridge—a town that seemed to hold very little of interest. There was one general store and a few small supply shops. Down the road was a church, a library, and a diner.

The autumn Minnesota winds chilled everyone to the bone. "I'm glad I bought those long johns," Aunt Alex observed.

Despite the underwear Barney was still cold—and tired, too. "Does your friend live far from here, Aunt Alex?"

"I'm not sure, dear, but Winnie will pick us up once she knows we've arrived. Let's call from that diner where we can all order hot drinks."

As they entered the diner, Aunt Alex hurried to the pay phone. When the waitress arrived, Crenshaw ordered two coffees, then went to wash his hands. Cassie and Barney were left alone to order their hot chocolate.

The waitress smiled at them. "You must be strangers in town. We don't get many strangers in these parts."

"We're visiting," explained Barney. "We've come to stay with Aunt Alex's friend, Winnie Comstock."

The waitress stopped smiling. "You kids are going out there—to the Comstock place?"

"Sure," said Barney.

The waitress looked frightened. "No one goes out there. Never."

"Why not?" asked Cassie.

"There are *wolves* out there," she said somberly. "Wolves roam wild on Comstock land. Killer wolves." She took their order, then quickly left.

Cassie stared at Barney. "Did she say *wolves*?"

"We must've misunderstood her."

Aunt Alex returned to the table. "Winnie is sending a friend to pick us up."

The waitress brought their order. "I knew Winnie Comstock wouldn't come herself," she said. "That woman *never* comes into this town, *never*." Her eyes had a strange, faraway look in them. "Not for more than a year."

Aunt Alex was concerned. "Why not? Has she been ill?"

The waitress had a fearful, glazed look in her eyes.

"Maybe you could call it that," she said, "but most folks call it something else." She placed the four cups on the table, then wiped her hands on her apron. "It's not my business and I always stick to my business." Nervously she tore the receipt from her pad and placed it on the table. "Pay at the cashier's," she said sharply, then walked away.

Crenshaw took his seat at the table.

"What do you make of that?" asked Aunt Alex. "That waitress seemed strange, Ollie. I think she's a little peculiar."

Barney agreed. "She told us there are *wolves* on Comstock property."

Aunt Alex looked surprised. "Wolves? That's nonsense."

Crenshaw wasn't so sure. "There are lots of wolves in northern Minnesota. It's one of their last refuges."

"Perhaps," said Aunt Alex, "but they can't be on Winnie's property."

As Cassie and Barney finished their hot chocolate, a leathery-faced old man wearing overalls and a windbreaker hurried into the diner. "I'm Farley Hooper," he explained. "Winnie sent me over. I've got my pickup parked out front, and I'm ready to take you to the Comstock place."

"Why didn't Winnie come herself?" asked Aunt Alex. "Is she ill?"

"She's fit as a fiddle," explained Farley. "The townsfolk don't like her, that's all."

Cassie stared at Aunt Alex. "You told us *everyone* liked Winnie Comstock."

"Never mind," said Aunt Alex. "Come, let's follow Mr. Hooper."

Outside, Farley Hooper's old pickup awaited them. It was a dilapidated old heap overflowing with junk. "There she is," he said proudly. "That's Daisy. Sorry for the mess, but Daisy isn't used to visitors."

Aunt Alex pushed aside a stack of birdseed, wire cables, and a tool chest, then crawled inside. "We don't mind," she said. "Come along, children, this is adventure riding."

Crenshaw brushed aside a pile of hay from the backseat. "I could forgo this adventure."

"This is fun," said Barney. "I'm glad we're out of that diner. I didn't like the crazy waitress."

Farley Hooper climbed into the driver's seat and quickly headed down the bumpy road. "You mean Sarah? She's not crazy."

"Yes, she is," Cassie explained. "She told us there are *wolves* on Winnie Comstock's land."

"She's absolutely right," Farley replied. "Hundreds of wolves live on Winnie's land. Out beyond her woods, must be more than a thousand wolves."

Cassie gasped. "Not real live vicious wild wolves!"

"That's right, girlie. But don't worry, you won't ever see them. Wolves live far away from people. Since the day Winnie arrived here, she's been protecting them."

Aunt Alex looked surprised. "Winnie always loved *dogs*, not wolves."

"People change," said Crenshaw. "Maybe your friend is a different person now. Living in the wilderness has probably made her *peculiar*."

"Or *insane*," Cassie added.

Farley Hooper steered to the left, barely missing another van. "I'll admit things haven't been the same since Winnie moved out here. First she bought up all those acres of good hunting land and turned it into a wildlife sanctuary. That got the locals stirred up. Then she'd fly to the state capitol to lobby for passage of the Endangered Species Act. That's what really riled people up. Up until then, there was a bounty of fifty dollars for each wolf slaughtered up here. Hunters did big business killing wolves."

"How did Winnie change that?" asked Aunt Alex.

"With the new law, hunters get a twenty-thousand-dollar fine or a year in jail if they're caught killing a wolf in these parts."

"Wolves are horrid creatures," said Cassie. "No one should *protect* them."

"Most folks agree," said Farley, "especially the cattle ranchers. It's a horrible sight to see a prize cow after a wolf attack—its head half hanging off, its guts eaten out."

Cassie was getting nauseated. She leaned her head out the window for some deep breaths of cold air.

"What's the matter, girlie? You look a little green."

"I feel sick," she said weakly.

"She's *scared*," teased Barney. "She's afraid a big, bad wolf will come along and eat her up."

"Don't joke like that," Aunt Alex scolded.

"Most everyone is afraid of wolves," said Farley reassuringly. "In fact, around here they're called the devil's dogs."

Barney leaned over toward Cassie. "The *devil's dogs*," he repeated mockingly.

Cassie shoved him away. "Don't push your luck, Prescott."

Up ahead, a large log cabin surrounded by a double row of Scotch pines began to emerge in the distance. "That's Winnie's place," shouted Farley. As he drove nearer, several large German shepherds leapt out from behind the trees and began barking furiously.

Cassie cringed in the seat. "It's a wolf attack!"

Barney laughed. "Those are only dogs, stupid."

"Pay them no mind," said Farley, "they're harmless as babies."

Crenshaw watched the dogs circle the truck as they

barked loudly. "They look decidedly vicious to me. I'm afraid to set foot out there!"

The dogs continued their threatening growls until Winnie Comstock hurried onto the porch to calm them down.

Aunt Alex waved excitedly. "Winnie looks so *different*, I hardly recognize her. She was always so plump and jolly."

Winnie Comstock had obviously changed. Her face was somber and haggard, with dark circles under her eyes. Her wiry gray-white hair flew wildly about her face as if it hadn't been combed for days. But when Winnie saw her old friend waving from the van, her face lit up with a smile. The smile quickly faded when she noticed Cassie and Barney. "You didn't tell me you were bringing *children*," she said with concern.

"I said I was bringing a *surprise*," said Aunt Alex. She rushed toward Winnie and gave her a bear hug.

Winnie seemed angry. "You shouldn't have brought *children*."

"Why not? You *love* children."

Winnie shook her head. "No, they don't belong *here*. Children snoop around, get into things."

"You'll love these two once you meet them," Aunt Alex insisted. "Cassie, Barney, say hello to my dear old friend. Come along, everyone, shake hands."

Reluctantly, Cassie stepped forward to shake Winnie's hand. But she drew back when she noticed Winnie's fingernails. Cassie had never seen nails so *long*.

Winnie looked embarrassed. She shoved her hands

into her pockets. "There's no beauty parlor out here," she explained. "It's been years since I had a decent manicure."

Barney was next to step from the van. "Don't you want us to stay here? My mom says I shouldn't stay where I'm not wanted."

Winnie's expression softened. "Of course I want you to stay. I'm hungry for visitors, *starving* for company. It gets mighty lonesome out here in the woods. I guess I thought you might be afraid."

"Afraid of what?" asked Barney.

Winnie shrugged. "Forget it, let's all go inside."

Cassie glanced at the large log cabin with its wrap-around porch. "I hope you have indoor plumbing."

Winnie looked amused. "I've a toilet and shower," she teased. "But if you want a bath, take it in the dam with the beavers."

Cassie gulped. "Are you *serious*?"

Aunt Alex laughed. "You've still got the same crazy sense of humor, old girl."

Winnie laughed, too. "It's going to be like old times, isn't it, Alex?"

Crenshaw climbed from the van, brushing strands of hay from his overcoat. "Have I been totally forgotten?"

"Of course not," said Aunt Alex. "Winnie, meet Ollie Crenshaw, my dear friend. He'll be tutoring the children during our visit."

Crenshaw glanced toward the house. "Are you sure there's room for us? Perhaps we'll go to a hotel."

Winnie shook her head. "The nearest hotel is probably in Minneapolis. You're all welcome, I've lots of room."

Farley Hooper helped Crenshaw carry the luggage into the house. As he hopped back into the van to drive off, Cassie rushed toward him. "I don't like this place," she confessed. "Are you sure we'll be *safe* here?"

"Of course you will, girlie," he reassured her. "Now that Winnie has company, she'll be just fine." Farley grabbed Cassie's arm. "A word of advice, though. Don't ever mention the *wolves*. That subject always makes Winnie go *crazy*!"

Farley Hooper waved good-bye and quickly drove away.

Chapter Four

WINNIE COMSTOCK'S LIVING ROOM WAS INVITING AND COZY. There were two large chintz-covered sofas in front of an open-hearth fireplace. Savory, tantalizing smells came wafting from the kitchen, reminding Barney of his mom's kitchen back home. Cassie was surprised to discover the place looked so homey.

"You must be hungry after your long journey," said Winnie. "I've food ready in the kitchen."

Maybe we could chow down outside?" suggested Barney. "It'd be like roughing it in the wilderness."

Crenshaw coaxed Barney toward the kitchen. "No, thank you, that's far too rustic for me."

A pot of beef stew was simmering on the stove and two deep-dish pies were cooling on the oven rack. As Winnie set down the plates on the checkerboard tablecloth, her hands began to tremble.

"Why are you so nervous?" asked Aunt Alex. "What's wrong?"

"Nothing's wrong," Winnie insisted. "I'm just jumpy lately. I suppose I've been alone out here too long."

"We'll cure that in no time," said Aunt Alex.

As everyone sat down at the table, Winnie dished out the stew. Most of the dinner conversation was between Winnie and Aunt Alex as they caught up on old times. Cassie remembered Farley Hooper's warning. She was careful not to bring up the subject of *wolves*, but she couldn't stop thinking about it.

When Winnie was about to serve the pie, Cassie noticed a movement outside the window. Suddenly a large, shadowy shape darted past. "There's an animal out there," she screamed.

"It's only a deer," explained Winnie. "I always set food out for them. They've grown so tame, they poke their noses right in the window."

"Are you sure?" Cassie asked.

Barney was nervous, too, but he wouldn't admit it. "Cassie is afraid it might be a *wolf*, come to eat her up."

Winnie dropped her fork. "A wolf?" she asked nervously. "Why did you say that? Who told you about the wolves?"

"Farley Hooper told us," said Aunt Alex. "He explained they live out beyond the woods. It isn't a secret, is it?"

"Of course not," Winnie replied. "I didn't mention it because of the children. Sometimes people get funny ideas. The wolves will never come near you. You won't even hear them howl unless you're deep in the woods."

"Are you absolutely sure?" asked Crenshaw. "I've no desire for wild encounters!"

"Relax," said Winnie, "the wolves are far away out in the forest, where they're safe." Her face grew grim. "But I'm afraid wolves will never be truly safe while people are around."

"I was speaking of *my own* safety," Crenshaw explained.

"Don't listen to foolish tales you hear in town," warned Winnie. "Folks around here don't like me, they never have. They'll be waiting to fill your heads with superstitious nonsense, but don't pay attention."

"Why do you like the wolves?" asked Barney. "Most people hate them."

Winnie's eyes filled with anger. "Only *ignorant* people hate wolves. In my lifetime, millions have been slaughtered."

"Millions?" asked Aunt Alex. "That's impossible."

"No, it's true," said Winnie. "Wolves have been strung up in trees and picked apart by pistol fire. Their dens have been dynamited and their mouths wired shut, causing them to starve. Wolves have been poisoned and shot down from helicopters. They've been doused with gasoline and ignited. Yes, all this has been done to the wolf and more. Then people call wolves bloodthirsty to justify their own savagery—the same people who hate and despise me for trying to protect them!"

Cassie nervously pushed her chair away from the table. Farley Hooper had been right: The subject of wolves definitely made Winnie Comstock crazy!

Barney was surprised at Winnie's emotional outburst.

"I'm sorry," she said, "wolves are a sensitive subject with me. It's not right to persecute any living creature." She leaned over and stared at Barney. "Do you know what it feels like to be caught in a trap? The pain is so severe, a wolf will chew off his own foot to escape it." Winnie began to clear the table. "Forget I said anything. I don't want you children upset while you're here. I assure you you're safe."

Cassie wasn't at all sure of that!

As night draped over the Minnesota woods, a dense blackness enveloped everything and a brisk wind rustled through the pine trees.

Inside the Comstock house the living room had a friendly aroma of burning logs and oiled cedar paneling. The German shepherds, bedded down for the night, curled up alongside one another on a large rag rug in the corner. The sounds of night owls mingled with the crackling of the popcorn kernels cooking inside the grating.

Winnie and her guests sat by the fireplace. At Aunt Alex's insistence, she was reciting poetry she'd written during long winter nights: "double-long-john nights," Winnie called them. The last embers of the fire faded away as she finished with a poem about wolves:

You know me not who see me not
My shape can shift and change.
Beneath the moon's bright vapors
I prowl a dwindling range.
Feared for my strength and majesty
Imprisoned from the sun
You know me not who see me not
But you and I are one.

Barney found the poem confusing. "How can you and the wolf be one?"

"The Indians tell us how," she explained. "They believed people were like wolves and that there's no real difference between the two. They felt we could blend into the wolf's spirit and *be* wolf."

Aunt Alex yawned. "I think we've had enough information for one night."

Winnie agreed. "You're right, it's sack-time."

"Sack-time?" asked Barney. "Does that mean we'll be sleeping in bags? That'd be just like camping out, wouldn't it?"

"Too much like it," Crenshaw observed.

"Don't worry, I've enough beds for everyone. C'mon, follow me."

Winnie led the way down the corridor toward the bedrooms. "My wiring is faulty, so you'll need oil lamps." She handed everyone a lamp from several that were on the hall table.

Aunt Alex opened the door to her bedroom. It was small but cozy. "I'll be asleep in no time," she said.

She kissed Winnie's cheek, then closed her bedroom door.

Barney wasn't eager to enter his room. There was something about it he didn't like: the heavy iron bars across the window. "What are those for?" he asked.

"They're in all the bedrooms," Winnie explained. "They were put in years ago before I bought the house."

Barney found that hard to believe.

"But they look *new*," he observed.

Winnie ignored his comment. "Sleep tight," she said, closing his door. "Don't let anything frighten you."

Cassie and Crenshaw were the last to be shown to their rooms. "Remember," Winnie said, "if you hear any strange sounds during the night, pay no attention."

"What kind of sounds?" asked Cassie.

Winnie didn't answer. She hurried down the hall toward her room and quickly closed the door.

Cassie found the house frightening at night. She was reluctant to enter her room, so she followed Crenshaw to his door. "Do you think it's safe to go to sleep in here?"

"What do you mean?" he asked suspiciously.

Cassie held out her oil lamp in the darkened hallway. "Do you think it's safe here?" she repeated somberly.

Crenshaw stared at Cassie, uncertain of what she meant. "I've read your file from cover to cover, young lady. I know all about your wicked pranks. But you won't burn this place down, no indeed." He took Cassie's oil lamp from her, then removed the matches from the hall table and placed them in his pocket. "*Now* I think it's safe to go to sleep! I'll see you in the morning," he declared, then slammed his door.

"I never burned down anything," said Cassie, vainly protesting her innocence to the closed door. Then her fear quickly turned to anger. "I hate you," she stated, "and I hate Aunt Alex and I hate my sappy cousin. And I won't stay in this house, I swear it!"

Soon after she'd gone to sleep, Cassie had a frightening nightmare. She dreamed she was locked inside a room with two vulture birds. One had the face of Mme. Fresnay and hovered overhead, scolding her. The other was her former classmate, Victoria Wembly. She had long, sharp red talons and fluttered about spitting flames from her beak.

Cassie woke up in a panic. For a moment she thought she was back in boarding school—the scapegoat for Victoria's nasty pranks again—being blamed for Victoria's vicious deeds as usual. "Sicky-Vicky" (as Cassie called her) was actually to blame for almost burning down the dormitory. But Cassie had been blamed—as always. Two-faced Victoria *never* got caught at anything. But Cassie always got blamed for *everything*—the things she *had* done and the things she *hadn't*.

Cassie rubbed her eyes and checked the clock. It was two A.M. The house was dark and silent as a tomb. As Cassie tried returning to sleep she heard a strange sound from outside. It came from far away through the darkness. It was an eerie moaning, whimpering wail, which sent shivers up her spine. Was it an animal? No, it sounded like a *human*. The moan echoed through the woods for a moment, then all was silent.

Cassie glanced toward the barred window. The full moon cast a gray-white glow across the pine trees. She tiptoed toward the dresser drawer and removed her purse. She checked the contents. Inside was two months' allowance, her escape money. She hurried back to bed and slipped the purse beneath her pillow. When the time was right, she'd make a quiet getaway, she told herself, then yawned.

Cassie had almost fallen asleep again when she heard the porch door slam. Then footsteps hurried down the hall. Someone had been out in the woods in the dead of night and was returning. Who could it be? Cassie knew it must be Winnie Comstock. Anyone else would have set the dogs howling.

Why would Winnie Comstock prowl around at night? she wondered.

Barney's mother always told him he "slept as soundly as a sweet potato." But Barney's first night in Winnie Comstock's house was a restless one. His analytical mind could think of only one reason to install iron bars on bedroom windows: to keep out something *wild* and *vicious*. That thought disturbed him so, he couldn't get to sleep.

Barney tossed restlessly. At two A.M. he was wide-awake when the strange moaning wail echoed from outside. Barney also heard the sound of someone sneaking back into the house soon after that. He, too, reasoned it had to be Winnie Comstock.

Why would Winnie be outside so late? he wondered.

Barney didn't know it, but across the hall in the opposite bedroom, Cassie was wondering exactly the same thing.

Chapter Five

AUNT ALEX WAS STANDING ON THE PORCH, WEARING A sweat suit and jogging shoes. As she began her morning exercises, Cassie and Barney stumbled toward her. "You two look exhausted this morning. Didn't you get any sleep?"

"Not much," said Barney. "Did you sleep okay?"

"Naturally," said Aunt Alex, beginning her knee bends. "Eight glasses of water each day and eight hours sleep each night can make a person live forever!" She took several deep breaths. "Suck in that air, children, it'll put roses in your cheeks."

"Did you hear anything strange last night?" asked Barney.

"Not a thing." Aunt Alex noticed Barney looked worried. "Did you hear something that frightened you?"

Barney wouldn't admit being frightened, especially not in front of Cassie. "I didn't hear anything."

Aunt Alex noticed Cassie looked worried, too. "Did *you* hear something strange last night?"

Cassie wouldn't admit being frightened, either. "Nothing."

"Then why do you both look so glum?" asked Aunt Alex. "It must be hunger. Crenshaw and Winnie went down to the lake to catch some fish. How about a good old-fashioned fish fry for breakfast?"

"I hate fish," said Cassie, "especially for breakfast."

"I love fish," said Barney, "anytime. It'll be like camping out."

Cassie glanced down the road toward the woods. She longed to be off on her own. She wanted privacy to plan her escape.

Aunt Alex pointed down the road. "Here comes Winnie. Doesn't she look perky this morning?"

Winnie Comstock looked much more cheerful than she had the day before. There was color in her cheeks and a smile on her face. As she rushed up the path her German shepherds barked and yapped at her heels, trying desperately to grab the two large fish she was carrying. She proudly held up her catch. "The big ones are jumping this morning. Crenshaw is on his way back with *five*. Who'll help me clean them?"

"I'm going for a walk," said Cassie.

"Is it safe for the children to wander where they like?" asked Aunt Alex.

"Certainly, all my land is posted," Winnie explained. "The only hunter on Comstock land is Fred Wicks. He rents a cabin down by the lake, but he can't hunt on *my* property. If I'd known he was a hunter, I never would've rented to him. I *hate* hunters." Winnie placed the fish on the porch table. "Professor Baxter rents the other cabin down there. It's a nice walk to the lake this time of day. Don't bother about the snakes, they're all harmless."

"Snakes?" asked Cassie. She was no longer eager to walk *alone*.

"You children go for a walk together," Aunt Alex suggested. "You'll work up a good appetite and get better acquainted."

The burnished autumn leaves crunched underfoot as Cassie and Barney walked through the woods toward the lake.

"According to the geography book," said Barney teasingly, "there's one *poisonous* variety of snake here. It's called the timber rattlesnake."

"Who cares?" said Cassie coolly.

"Don't you want to know what it looks like?"

"Okay, what?"

"I'm not telling."

"You're totally *juvenile!*"

Barney gloated as he watched Cassie tiptoe cautiously through the fallen leaves. "You're totally *scared*. Now it's your turn to worry about being poisoned. How's it feel?"

Cassie stopped in her tracks. "Let's get things straight, Prescott. We don't like each other, right?"

"True."

"So let's just shut up and walk, okay?" Cassie gasped as a rabbit suddenly darted across the path. She feared each new sound in the shrubbery might be a timber rattlesnake, and she was furious at Barney for placing the idea in her head.

As they approached the lake, a flock of mallard ducks flew overhead, and Barney spotted several beavers in a dam nearby. There were two cabins beside the lake. Outside one, a man dressed in hunting gear sat polishing his rifle. As several ruffled grouse fluttered above the edge cover near the woods' opening, he got up, about to cock the trigger. When he saw Cassie and Barney approach, he quickly put down the rifle. "Did you see that?" he asked. "Fool hens, we hunters call them. There's a whole flock of them in the brush there. It's just like shooting fish in a barrel to pick them off."

"You're not allowed to shoot anything here," said Barney. "Winnie Comstock said so."

The man grew angry. "I know that. No need for that Comstock woman to send spies down here to check up on me."

"We're not spies, we're guests," said Barney.

"Guests? Who're you kidding? Winnie Comstock never has guests. *No one* comes around her place. My name is Wicks. I rent this cabin, but I've never seen anyone up at the big house. That's because no one likes Winnie Comstock around these parts."

"So I've heard," said Cassie.

"Have you heard she likes *wolves*?" he asked.

"I'm afraid so," Cassie replied.

Wicks nodded. "Yeah, there's something unnatural about the way that woman protects those devil's dogs. Hounds straight from hell, that's what they are. In the old days I used to make a mighty good living hunting down those creatures. But those were the good old bounty days before Winnie's kind spoiled everything. Us hunters were of value then. The cattle ranchers couldn't do without us. But now those beasts can roam and kill at will. It's criminal the way the law protects those killers!" Fred Wicks placed his gun on his lap to oil the handle. "A wolf hunter was *respected* in the old days," he continued. "It's not the same anymore. There's not enough deer around to make a living with the wolves killing them all." Anger and resentment filled Wicks's eyes as he rubbed the handle harder. "Folks in town don't like it, no sir. Some won't let their kids wait for the school bus. They're afraid a wolf might come and snatch them."

"Could that really happen?" asked Cassie.

"Anything can happen with wolves around," said Fred Wicks. "How long are you kids staying?"

"We don't know," said Barney.

Fred Wicks stared down the barrel of his rifle. "I'm warning you, be on your guard. Strange things go on in these woods, especially at *night*."

"What kind of things?" asked Barney.

"Eerie, unnatural things," he explained solemnly. "*Evil* things. I'm warning you, this is no place for children." He propped his rifle on his shoulder. "One more warning: Stick together." Then he walked off down the road toward the forest.

As Cassie watched Fred Wicks leave she thought of the eerie sound she'd heard in the night. Was that part of the "evil" he warned about? She longed to confide in Barney, to admit she was scared, but she'd made him her enemy. Cassie would never admit weakness to an enemy!

Barney, too, wondered silently. Did evil things go on in the woods at night? He kicked at some dried leaves. "What do you think of that guy? Kind of creepy, isn't he?"

Cassie continued walking. "Not half as creepy as *you*," she stated. As she neared the opposite side of the lake, she became aware of a dreadful odor. "What's that?" she asked, sniffing. Barney noticed it, too. The awful stench was coming from outside the second cabin.

As they approached, they noticed a heavy iron kettle on the porch with a fire burning beneath it. Curious, Barney looked inside. Gray sludgy scuzz covered the top of the boiling water. The horrible stink nearly knocked him over.

A man ran from the cabin carrying a wooden spoon. He had bright red hair, a thick beard, and even thicker glasses. "Careful, don't touch that," he cautioned. He vigorously stirred the contents of the kettle. "Pretty putrid, isn't it?"

"What's in there?" Cassie asked.

"It's a stew," he replied. "A few dozen mice, a few squirrels, some muskrat, skunk, and raccoon. It's part of my experiment for the University in Minneapolis. Whatever dead animal I find goes right into the pot."

Cassie backed away. "How disgusting."

"All in the name of science," he explained. "I'm Professor Horace Baxter, a biologist at the university. When these skeletons are boiled down, they'll make marvelous specimens. This is an adjunct to my research on wolves. We still know so little about the wolf diet. Whenever I come across a dead wolf, I examine the remains in its stomach to make comparisons."

"That's truly gross," Cassie said.

"No, it's fascinating," Professor Baxter said. "Of course, I'm not usually lucky enough to find a dead wolf in the forest. I've only rudimentary equipment in my cabin, but it's enough." The professor seemed eager to share his research. "Would you like to see my makeshift laboratory?"

"No," Cassie said.

"Yes," Barney said, then followed the professor inside.

In a corner of the kitchen, Professor Baxter proudly displayed the contents of his traveling laboratory. Barney was fascinated by the collection of glittering scalpels, brain spoons, bone shears, and other intricate equipment used to conduct autopsies on dead wolves.

"I've come to regard the wolf as a marvelously resourceful animal," the professor explained. When he can't catch cows, deer, or sheep, he'll eat sparrows, beetles, spiders, ants, even fruits and vegetables. I've found some fascinating contents inside a wolf's stomach."

"Have you found any *children*?" Cassie asked.

"No, there's never been evidence of a timber wolf killing a human in these woods. Of course, legends of *versipellis* still linger on around here, but that's all superstition."

"What's *versipellis*?" Barney asked.

"Never mind," said Baxter. "I'm a scientist and we don't believe in legends. *Facts* are our stock in trade."

Outside, the odor from Professor Baxter's "stew" was making Cassie nauseous. "I think we should leave now," she said.

"Would you like some tea before you go?" he asked. "I also have some nice black bean soup."

Cassie glanced at the stove. The wretched mess bubbling in the pot smelled almost as bad as the wretched mess boiling outside. "No, thanks," she said.

Barney noticed Cassie's queasy expression.

"We're having fish for breakfast," he added. "*Fried* fish."

Cassie's stomach gurgled uneasily as she hurried from the cabin.

Chapter Six

THE DAY WENT STEADILY DOWNHILL FOR CASSIE. DESPITE her protests, Aunt Alex insisted she eat some fish. "It's brain food," she explained. This evoked several nasty comments from Barney. When the meal was over, Cassie and Barney drew straws for cleaning detail. Cassie lost. She spent the next half hour in the kitchen, washing up.

In the afternoon, Crenshaw made the children hike outdoors, then gave them a botany lesson. To make things worse, Barney seemed to enjoy it all. Cassie wasn't sure Barney was having a good time or only just pretending to spite her, which drove her nutty.

After dinner, Cassie sat glumly leafing through an outdated issue of *Natural History* magazine. She saw pictures of buffaloes and bears, but not one pair of Gucci boots. While Aunt Alex and Crenshaw played

Scrabble with Barney, she yawned and stared at the moose head above the mantel.

With the darkness, Cassie's uneasiness about Winnie Comstock returned. Winnie seemed to act differently after dark. Her eyes widened like a cat's about to pounce and she paced the room like a caged animal.

"Winnie, come play Scrabble with us," Aunt Alex suggested.

Winnie settled down for a game, but she still seemed preoccupied.

"You come play, too," Aunt Alex told Cassie.

"No, thanks, I'm not good at word games."

"I'm *great* at them," Barney boasted. "Once I hear a word I never forget it."

Crenshaw agreed. "Barney remembered the names of all the trees I taught him today."

Aunt Alex smiled. "Very commendable."

"Cassie couldn't remember any," Barney added.

Aunt Alex sipped her tea. "This herbal tea is wonderful, Winnie. What's in it?"

"A special ingredient," Winnie replied. Her mind wasn't on the game. She kept glancing toward the window, as if waiting for something.

Barney arranged the letters on the Scrabble board to form a word.

Aunt Alex stared at it. "Don't cheat, young man. You can't make up words."

"I didn't make it up," Barney said. "It's a real word. Professor Baxter used it this morning."

"I've never heard it," Aunt Alex said. She stared

43

down at the letters, then spelled them out loud. *"V-E-R-S-I-P-E-L-L-I-S.* That sounds like nonsense."

Winnie stared down at the Scrabble board. Then her face suddenly turned as white as a sheet.

"Barney is correct," Crenshaw explained. *"Versipellis* is a Latin word."

"Are you sure?" Aunt Alex asked. "Let's look it up in the dictionary."

The suggestion upset Winnie.

"No!" she shouted. "Don't you dare look up that word!"

Aunt Alex seemed surprised. "Why not?"

Winnie calmed herself. "The dictionary doesn't list Latin words."

"No matter," Crenshaw said. "I remember its meaning. Roughly translated, it means turn-pelt."

"And what does that mean?" Aunt Alex asked.

Crenshaw explained. "A turn-pelt is a human who can change into . . ."

Winnie jumped up from her seat as if a fit had come over her.

"Lies!" she shouted. "All lies!" Then with a sweep of her hand, she knocked all the letters off the board. "Latin words don't count. Besides, it's getting too late for games. We should all go to bed."

Everyone looked surprised. Aunt Alex stared at her old friend. "Winnie, what's wrong?"

Winnie struggled to calm herself.

"Nothing. When you live in the woods you have to wake up with the birds. No city-slicker habits out here, you know." She poured Crenshaw and Aunt Alex more tea. "Drink up, then we'll all go to bed."

By now Cassie was certain Winnie was hiding something dark and sinister. She vowed not to stay in her house another night.

As soon as everyone had gone to bed, Cassie promised herself she'd run away.

As Cassie sat in her room that night, she realized she had a problem. Only a fool would venture into the woods at night alone, and she was no fool.

Cassie also realized there was only one solution to her problem. Barney Prescott was a wimpy weasel, but he wasn't afraid of snakes and he loved the outdoors.

Somehow, Cassie had to convince him to go with her!

Barney was half asleep when he heard the tap at his door.

"Let me in," the voice whispered.

"Who's out there?"

"It's me, Cassie. Let me in."

"Not by the hair of my chinny-chin-chin!"

"Quit joking and open up."

Barney opened the door. Cassie was dressed in her boots and parka. "You must be awfully cold," he joked.

"Keep your voice down, Prescott." Cassie pushed him back into the room, then closed the door.

"What do you want?"

"I'm here to do you a big favor. I'm leaving this place tonight."

"Leaving? Where are you going?"

"Not so loud," Cassie cautioned, "you'll wake everyone."

Barney lowered his voice. "Why are you leaving?"

"I can't stand this place," Cassie said. "Winnie Comstock is weird. I'm sure she's hiding some horrible secret. I've got enough money to get me far away from here, so I'm leaving."

"You can't run away," Barney argued.

Cassie sat down on the edge of Barney's bed and crossed her legs confidently. "Why not? I *always* run away. So far, I've run away from three boarding schools. Once when I ran away in Paris I stayed at a hotel for two days before I was found. Running away is fun. It certainly beats hanging around here with a *crazy* person."

"Do you think Winnie Comstock is crazy?" Barney asked.

"Anyone who loves wolves must be insane," Cassie said. "I heard her sneaking around last night. And I heard groans outside like someone was being tortured."

"I heard that, too," Barney said. "What do you think Winnie was doing outside so late?"

"Something awful, I'm sure. Fred Wicks warned us about evil doings, remember?"

"That's right!"

"He also told us to stick together," Cassie added coyly. "That's why I've decided to take you with me."

46

"You want *me* to come along?"

Cassie was thrilled her plan was working. Barney seemed *flattered*. "I admit you'll be underfoot and in my way," she said grandly. "You've got no style, Prescott, no joie de vivre. You've probably got no money, either; but we're related, so I can't leave you behind. That path through the woods leads straight into town, I'm sure. From there we can hitch a ride into the city. We'll be hours away before anyone knows we're gone."

"Hitchhiking?"

"Sure, it's a fun way to travel. You said you liked fun and adventure."

For a moment Barney didn't say anything. Then he began to figure things out. "Who're you kidding?"

"What do you mean?" Cassie asked innocently.

"You must think I'm awful dumb. You haven't said one decent word to me since we met, so who're you kidding? You're *afraid* to go alone."

"I'm not afraid of anything."

"Yes, you are," Barney said smugly. "You're scared. And you're thoughtless, too. Aunt Alex would have a fit if she found us gone."

"You're even wimpier than I thought," Cassie said. "You haven't figured anything out yet, have you? You're a *charity case*, Prescott. Aunt Alex feels sorry for you because your family is poor. She took pity on you."

"That's a lie! Aunt Alex never said that."

"Then Aunt Alex lied, not me," Cassie protested. "Judge for yourself. She told us we'd have a great time

47

here; that's a lie. She said Winnie Comstock had lots of friends; that's sure a lie. Adults lie all the time."

"No, they don't."

"Yes, they do, I should know. My parents make a career of lying to me! Every time they switch me to a new school they tell me it'll be wonderful, but it's always awful. And every time they promise to visit me, they never show up. They're always too busy. Adults are *always* lying."

"You're trying to trick me," Barney said, "but forget it, I'm not going with you."

Cassie grabbed him by the shoulders. "Now I get it. You're smarter than I thought, Prescott. Okay, how much?"

"What?"

"How much do you want? Twenty dollars? Thirty? It's okay, I'm used to buying people. I told you, I've lots of money, so it's no problem. I once gave Cynthia Houseman fifty dollars so she'd invite me to her party."

"That's disgusting!"

"Maybe so. It turned out to be a dreadful party."

"No, *you're* disgusting," Barney explained. He pushed her away. "You're real pathetic. If you weren't so mean, I'd feel sorry for you."

Cassie's face grew red-hot. "Take that back," she shouted. "Don't you dare say that. Don't you ever feel sorry for me!"

Pity was the one thing Cassie wouldn't tolerate. In the first year she'd spent at boarding school, when she was six, classmates had felt sorry for her because her parents never visited. Cassie had acted mean and spiteful to avoid their pity. She'd continued being mean and spiteful ever since. "*No one* needs to feel sorry for me," she repeated. To her horror, she felt herself about to cry. She turned away, then hurried toward the door. "Stay here if you like, see if I care. I'm leaving and I never want to see your sappy face again."

"You're bluffing," Barney said. "You're afraid to go by yourself."

Cassie's voice began to tremble. "No, I'm not. I'm getting out of here right now and I'm going *alone*." She flung open the door and hurried out into the hall.

Barney scratched his head. Were *all* girls such a pain? he wondered.

Chapter Seven

CASSIE FOUGHT BACK HER TEARS AS SHE RAN DOWN THE darkened road toward the woods. The thin sliver of moonlight emerging from the trees was her only light. Anger burned inside her as she reached the end of the clearing, then raced down the narrow path etched between the trees.

Cassie hurried faster, ignoring her direction. She was determined to escape. It wasn't long before she realized she was *lost*. Cassie couldn't find the path toward the lake that she and Barney had taken earlier. In the darkness she couldn't find her way at all. She was stuck somewhere in the woods with no idea how to get out.

Cassie panicked. She ran even faster. And as she ran she became gripped by the fear that someone, or something, was following her.

50

Then Cassie stopped. She'd heard a skittering noise in the dense, dark underbrush behind her. Yes, something was definitely following her! As she began to run again, she heard *it* running along behind her. When she slowed down, *it* slowed its pace as well.

Suddenly the unknown thing in the darkness began to moan. The moan was followed by a cry that echoed through the trees. Cassie stopped. She heard the cry again. Whatever was pursuing her, it was awfully close.

Cassie didn't know which way to turn. She paused again, gasping for breath. Suddenly she heard a voice call out through the darkness: "Where are you?"

It was a *familiar* voice. "Barney, is that you?" Cassie called out.

"Who else?" Barney moaned. "Come help me. I'm stuck in the brambles."

Cassie hurried toward the sound of Barney's voice. She was never so happy to see anyone.

"Help me out of here!" Barney shouted. He tugged at his robe, which had become entangled in the brambles.

Cassie tried to pull him out. As she did, she ripped off the side of his flannel robe.

"Now look what you've done," he complained.

"You told me to help you get loose. What are you doing stuck in there anyway?"

"Chasing *you*, of course. But every time I'd get close, you'd run ahead."

"I didn't know it was *you* chasing me," Cassie argued. "Why didn't you say so, birdbrain?"

51

"I never thought you'd have the nerve to get this far," Barney explained.

"I told you I wasn't scared."

Barney plucked some thorns from his robe. "You might've fallen down a gopher hole or something. Dumb girls can't handle themselves in the outdoors."

"Look who's talking," Cassie teased. "You're the one with all the prickles."

"Sure, be nasty. Why are you always so nasty?"

"Why'd you follow me?"

"To rescue you, dummy. It was awful stupid of you to come in here. Fred Wicks warned us it wasn't safe in the woods at night."

"Why'd you want to rescue me?" asked Cassie suspiciously. "I'll bet *you* think something weird is going on around here, too."

"What if I do?"

"And you're *scared*," Cassie said. "I'll bet that's why you followed me. You're afraid to be left alone back there, admit it."

"I'll admit it if you will," Barney said.

"I won't admit anything!"

"Then neither will I!" Barney said firmly. "I'm heading back to the house. Go into town if you want, I won't stop you."

"I don't know the way to town," Cassie confessed.

"I don't know the way back to the house," Barney admitted.

"Swell, then we're lost!"

"I guess we *should* stick together."

"Do you think we'll freeze out here?" Cassie asked.

Barney pulled his parka tighter. "I'll freeze first, I'm in my pajamas. I never should've run after you."

"If you hadn't made me so angry, I never would've come in here. Only an idiot runs into the woods alone!"

"So you *were* trying to trick me into coming with you. Of all the mean, sneaky, slimy . . ."

"That doesn't matter now," Cassie said. "Let's hang close together and hope we're going in the right direction."

"What if it's the *wrong* direction? In case you've forgotten, there are *wolves* out there in the forest. What if . . ."

A piercing howl came from somewhere beyond the trees. It was a full-throated, semi-human sound, combining the most primitive elements of man and beast. The eerie cry shattered the stillness of the woods.

Barney froze in his tracks. "That's the same sound I heard last night."

"Yes, that's what I heard, too. Do you think it's a wolf?"

"I'm not sure what it is. Or *where* it is," Barney said.

The ominous howl seemed to come from everywhere at once, echoing through the trees on either side of the woods.

"Which way should we run?" Cassie asked helplessly. "I think we're doomed!"

"Whatever that thing is, it sounds hungry," Barney observed.

Cassie grabbed his arm. "I can almost see it out

there," she whimpered. "It has huge jaws and huge claws and huge teeth and it's waiting to pounce."

"Let's pray it doesn't see us."

The clouds that had been covering the moon suddenly lifted and passed over. The moonlight clearly illuminated the path where Cassie and Barney stood cringing in fear. They were now easy prey for a prowling beast on the loose.

With the added light, Barney noticed something. A figure stood silhouetted off in the distance. "Look, we're not alone in here," he said with relief. "Someone else is in the woods. Let's run and ask for help."

As Barney hurried toward the figure up ahead, Cassie followed. "Who could it be?" she asked. "Do you think it's Fred Wicks? If it is, I hope he has his rifle with him."

"Sure, it's probably Wicks," said Barney, hurrying faster. "Only a hunter would dare come into the woods at night."

"Shout for help," Cassie said. "Let him know we're here."

Barney was about to call out to let Fred Wicks know they were coming. Suddenly he realized the figure up ahead wasn't Fred Wicks, after all. By the light of the moon that filled the clearing, Barney could see the figure staring off toward the forest.

"Look, it's Winnie Comstock," Barney said.

Cassie pushed him aside to take a look. "You're right. Maybe this is where she was last night, too. What do you suppose she's doing here?"

Cassie and Barney hurried toward Winnie. Then they stopped dead in their tracks. Once again they heard the horrible inhuman howl—only this time they knew exactly where it was coming from.

It was coming from Winnie Comstock!

As Winnie stood in the clearing, she opened her mouth and the horrid sound poured forth.

"What's she doing?" Cassie gasped.

"She's baying at the moon," Barney said, "just like a *wolf*!"

Chapter Eight

"WHAT A STUPID, PINHEADED, BRAINLESS THING TO DO!"
Cassie threw her parka onto Barney's bed. "Why'd we
come back here?"

Barney hurried to the drawer. He grabbed a pair of
heavy woolen socks and slipped them on. "Did you
have a better idea? You should've thanked me for
finding the way back."

"I didn't want to come back," Cassie whined.

"Too bad," Barney said. "Even if I knew the way to
town, I wouldn't have gone in my pajamas. People
would think I'm nuts."

"Speaking of nuts, what should we do about Winnie?
Which one of us should tell Aunt Alex her friend is
bonkers?"

"Don't jump to conclusions," Barney said. "Maybe
there's an explanation for what we saw tonight."

"Like what?"

56

Barney pulled on his sheepskin slippers. "Winnie could've had a bad toothache or something. After all, I groaned pretty loud when I got stuck in the brambles."

"Don't be a twit, Prescott. That's stupid, and you know it."

"Well, I'm not telling Aunt Alex her friend is screwy," he protested. "Let's tell Crenshaw instead. Why don't *you* tell him?"

"I can't," Cassie explained. "Crenshaw doesn't trust me. He's already accused me of trying to burn this house down."

"Really?"

"Absolutely. He wouldn't believe a word I said."

"I mean, were you really going to? Burn this place down?"

"Maybe," Cassie said slyly. "*You'll* never know, that's for sure." She paced the room, then sighed. "Let's face it, we can't tell anyone. Adults never believe what kids say, anyway. They'll think we had a nightmare or something."

For once Barney agreed with Cassie. "Maybe if we had some proof," he suggested.

Cassie heard a noise on the porch. She hurried toward the door to listen. "We don't want Winnie to know we're awake," she cautioned. "She mustn't find out we saw her in the woods."

Barney put his ear against the door, too. They heard Winnie walk past the room, down the hall toward her bedroom. Then she closed her door behind her.

"Maybe it's safe to leave now," said Cassie. She

opened the door and poked her head out to glance around. "Look, Barney," she said, staring down at the hall rug. There was a large, moist red stain seeping into the carpeting.

"That's *blood*," said Barney. "Fresh blood. Do you suppose Winnie got hurt?"

Next to the stain lay a torn piece of yellow plaid flannel. "That's part of the shirt Winnie was wearing tonight," said Cassie. She pointed down at the carpet. "But I can't imagine what *that thing* is a part of."

Cassie and Barney stared down at the sinister object. Beside the torn shirt remnant lay the bloodied claw of an unidentified *animal*.

With the coming of sunrise, the house seemed warm and cozy again. The German shepherds were yapping by the porch door, pleading to be let out for their morning run. Winnie was in the kitchen. The aroma of fresh biscuits and scrambled eggs filled the air.

Cassie and Barney stood in the kitchen doorway. "Winnie looks perfectly normal this morning," Cassie observed.

"It must have something to do with the full moon," Barney reasoned. "Maybe she's normal during the day, then goes nuts at night."

How nuts? Cassie wondered, thinking of the animal claw they'd discovered. "Where do you suppose that claw came from?" she asked. "What do you think it has to do with Winnie?"

Winnie noticed the children staring at her from the

doorway. "Look at the early birds," she said, smiling. She bent over the oven and removed a trayful of buttermilk biscuits, then hurried toward the cupboard for a jar of homemade raspberry jam. "I had a wonderful berry season this year, and I put up twenty pints."

As Winnie closed the cupboard, Cassie gasped and stared at her hands. She noticed one of Winnie's long fingernails was gone. It had been broken off!

Barney was starving. He gobbled down the eggs and drizzled jam along the biscuits. When Aunt Alex came down to breakfast she was thrilled to see his hearty appetite. "That's more like it. A good night's sleep and a good breakfast will help you live forever."

Crenshaw came to the table yawning. "I certainly slept well. The moment my head hit the pillow, I was out. *Nothing* could've woken me up last night."

"You'll always sleep soundly in this house," Winnie said firmly. "I'll personally make sure of that."

Cassie had a disturbing thought. She nudged Barney and whispered in his ear. "Do you suppose Winnie drugged that tea last night?"

Winnie offered the biscuit tray to Barney. "Have another. I put in a secret ingredient."

Barney pushed his plate aside. "I don't want any more."

Aunt Alex laughed. "I'm not surprised. Three helpings should suffice until lunch."

"We're having a very special lunch," Winnie explained. "Professor Baxter is coming and I'm making my fa-

59

mous dill potatoes with fresh herbs. I grow all my own herbs."

Barney excused himself and carried his plate to the sink. Cassie followed. "We have to speak to Professor Baxter," Barney said as he rinsed off the dishes.

"You're right," Cassie agreed. "The word he used yesterday was the one that upset Winnie last night. It could be a clue."

"Either Winnie is crazy or she's hiding some awful secret. Maybe Baxter knows which."

Cassie watched as Winnie walked toward the window herb garden to pick some dill. "Until we find out which, I'm not eating her food, that's for sure."

Winnie turned sharply and glanced at the children with a threatening expression. "What are you two whispering about?" she asked suspiciously. "Stop it, I hate whispering!"

Chapter Nine

LATER THAT MORNING FARLEY HOOPER DROVE UP, LOUDLY honking his horn. "Hi, kids, how about a ride into town? I'll show you the sights of Blue Ridge."

Cassie put down the botany book she was studying. "This is the perfect opportunity to *escape*," she whispered. "Once we're in town, we can hitchhike out of here just as I planned."

"I'm no *coward*," said Barney. "Something weird is happening here, and I'm sticking around to discover what's up. Besides, I wouldn't leave Aunt Alex. I *like* Aunt Alex."

Cassie wouldn't admit it, but she liked Aunt Alex, too. "I'm not a coward, either," she said. "If you stay, I'll stay."

Farley honked the horn again. "How's about it? You two coming or what?"

Cassie waved and threw the book aside. "I'll be right

61

there," she called. "If I don't spend some money soon, I'll burst."

"Wait," said Barney. "Can you be trusted? What if you're planning to run away *without* me?"

Cassie loved Barney's uncertainty about her.

"That's possible," she said smugly. "Get this straight, Prescott, I never promise anyone anything—*never*—got it?" Then she hurried toward the van.

Barney hurried after her. "I'm coming, too."

They hopped into the old pickup, which went bumping along the back roads. When Farley pulled into Blue Ridge he headed for the feed store. "I'll meet you kids by the library in an hour, okay?"

Cassie glanced around. "What I wouldn't give for a decent boutique," she said, sighing.

Barney pointed to Larsen's Emporium. "Let's try that place."

The Emporium was a combination five-and-dime/general store, specializing in handmade rustic items. As Cassie went looking for "fashion treasures," Barney strolled around.

At a potbellied stove in the corner, two of the local hunters were playing checkers by a folding table. They were dressed in high rubber boots and old khakis and were arguing with each other.

"Come off it, Sam. For shooting through brush you need at least a thirty caliber to drop a white-tailed deer."

"Hold on, Jack, who said you didn't?" Sam shouted back. "I'm only saying you don't need a big-bore every time. In a blowdown, a Magnum cartridge is a waste because any bullet turns into a brush-cutter. I save my high-power stuff for moose. When I'm hunting white-tails, I just bring my hounds. Those bucks leave so many rubs and scrapes on the trees, the hounds can sniff 'em out real easy."

Jack pushed his checker piece along the board. "Sure, Sam, hounds are real good for close range, but only when you're using buckshot. Now, moose are a different story."

"Didn't I just say that?" Sam argued. He made a move, capturing two of his opponent's kings. "Of course, in the old days, you could pick off those thousand-pound bulls all along the timberline and you didn't need no high-caliber stuff, neither, no sir."

The two men looked up and noticed Barney. "Hi there, sonny," Sam said. He smiled, revealing a mouthful of yellow teeth. "I haven't seen your face around here before."

"I'm new in town," said Barney. "I'm visiting."

"How about a game?" asked Jack. "In the old days kids were always hanging around here looking for a hot checker game."

"And a good hunting story," Sam added. "Yes, sir, the young ones would always hang around here after school, remember? Fred Wicks always had the best stories."

"I know Fred Wicks," Barney said.

Sam nodded. "Then you must know Fred was the best hunter-trapper in these parts. He could kill a wolf quicker than look at it. He'd drop hundreds each year and have pelts hanging up every which way."

"True enough," Jack said. "I remember Fred once got a gold watch from the county for killing old Three Toes by Beaver Creek. For six years, a hundred and fifty men tried capturing that killer wolf. Fred finally got 'im."

Sam leaned back in his chair, his hands behind his head. "Things were real lively in those days, but no more. Now when the young ones finish school they all go off to the big cities. No one wants to listen to hunting stories no more."

Barney felt sorry for the two old hunters, but he wanted to keep an eye on Cassie. He suspected she was still planning to run away.

But Cassie had other things on her mind. She was strolling down the aisles, admiring the shelves of home-made preserves, relishes, and ciders, and wheels of local cheeses. The gourmet goodies reminded her of Harrods department store in London.

Down the center aisle, Cassie found quilts, embroidered baby clothing, and fancy knit items. "What lovely things," she said admiringly. "Cottage industry items are real high fashion now. It's strictly de rigueur to have at least one handmade item in one's wardrobe." Cassie held up an oversized woolen sweater with a red-and-white reindeer pattern. "What do you think?"

Barney shrugged.

She held up the same sweater in a blue-and-white design. "Which looks better?"

Barney shrugged again.

"Okay, I'll buy them both." Cassie also selected two hand-knit scarves and some gloves. She brought the items to the cashier, who politely wrapped her purchases. "That wipes me out," she said, "but it's worth it."

The cashier smiled. "Hi, I'm Cora Larsen, the owner. It's always nice to meet new customers. Come again, honey."

"I will," Cassie said. "We're staying at the Comstock place, and we'll come back."

The color suddenly drained from Cora Larsen's face. "The Comstock place?" she asked. "No, you can't be staying *there*. You kids aren't safe there. Everyone knows Winnie Comstock's place is dangerous." Cora hurried toward the two hunters, who were still arguing over their game. "These kids are staying at the Comstock place. Tell them what you found by the woods near there last night."

Jack dropped his checker piece. "It was a horrible sight. I can't hardly say what kind of animal it was—a dog, maybe. It'd been ripped apart, limb from limb, claws scattered every which way."

Cassie shuddered, remembering the bloody claw she'd seen on the hall carpet. "How awful. Was it killed by a wolf?"

Jack shook his head. "No wolf kills like that. And no wolf leaves markings like the ones I saw. It was another kind of beast altogether."

"If it wasn't a wolf, what was it?" Barney asked.

Cora Larsen grabbed Barney's arm. "You mustn't stay out there, understand? The beast that prowls on Comstock land is no ordinary animal!"

"Hold on, Cora, you can't know that for sure," Sam argued.

"It's true just the same," she insisted.

"What sort of beast is it?" Cassie asked apprehensively.

Cora was growing frightened and refused to say more. "Just remember you've been warned." She noticed two customers waiting at the register. "Don't forget what I told you," she insisted as she left. "You kids get out of that place as fast as you can!"

Barney walked back toward the hunters. "What *beast* is she talking about?"

Sam pushed his chair closer to the stove. "Don't upset yourself, boy. It may be no more than a legend. Me, I've never seen it myself. But if it's anything like some folks tell, I hope I never do."

"Folks started speaking of it a while back," Jack added. "They say there's an animal that lives in the woods but it isn't an animal. Nonsense, most likely."

Sam glanced up as a tall, dark-haired man in a fur cap and leather jacket came down the aisle of the store. "That's Pierre," he explained. "Pierre doesn't think the legend is nonsense. He says he's *seen* the beast."

Cassie and Barney approached the stranger. "Have you seen the beast that lives in the woods out by the Comstock place?" Barney asked.

Fear sparkled in Pierre's dark-brown eyes. "That woods, she is bad." He had a thick French-Canadian accent, and his voice quivered nervously. "The loup-garou lives out there. Yes, I have seen with my eyes the loup-garou."

"Loup-garou?" Cassie asked. "What kind of animal is that?"

"The loup-garou, it is *evil*," Pierre insisted. "It is deadly."

"Can you show us where you saw it?" Barney asked.

Pierre grew petrified. "No, I never return there," he shouted. "No one is safe from the loup-garou." He made a symbolic sign in the air, then hurried out of the store.

Cassie was confused. "I've never heard of a loup-garou. What on earth could it be?"

"We've got to find out right away," Barney said. "If there's a beast in the woods, I want to know exactly what it is!"

"What are you doing?" Cassie asked.

Barney was thumbing through the index cards in the Blue Ridge library. "Looking for answers, of course."

"How can we find them *here*?"

"You can find everything in a library. If you'd read more, you'd know that." Barney pulled out another drawer. "Here it is. Loup-garou is listed under folklore."

Barney hurried toward the bookstacks. He ran his fingers over several titles until he found *Man's Myths and Symbols*. He brought the book to the checkout desk and filled out a temporary card. As the librarian stamped the book, Farley Hooper began honking his horn outside.

Cassie and Barney hurried toward the pickup. As usual, Farley had filled the back with stacks of meal, flour, seed, and other provisions, so they squashed themselves into a corner.

As they bumped along, Barney read through the book intently. Meanwhile, Cassie was growing more uneasy. "I shouldn't have bought these clothes," she grumbled. "Now I've no money left to run away. I guess I'm stuck at Winnie's place, like it or not."

Presently, Barney glanced up from the book with a solemn expression. "I've just discovered what *versipellis* and loup-garou mean."

"Good," said Cassie, "at least we'll solve a piece of this puzzle. What do they mean?"

"I'm afraid they're fancy words for werewolf."

"Werewolf?" Cassie gasped. "You mean Winnie has a werewolf living on her property? I can't believe it."

"I don't want to believe it either," said Barney, "but it solves part of the puzzle. At least now we know why no one likes her!"

Chapter Ten

CASSIE AND BARNEY HAD NO TIME TO DISCUSS THE STAR-tling news. As Farley came to a dead stop outside the Comstock house, they noticed the place was in a state of confusion. Fred Wicks was running from the porch with Professor Baxter trailing after him. Winnie, Aunt Alex, and Crenshaw were close behind.

"What's up?" Farley asked.

Crenshaw paused to explain. "Mr. Wicks discovered a most intriguing footprint in the woods. He insists the professor inspect it at once."

"What kind of print?" Barney asked.

"We'll soon find out," Crenshaw said.

Fred Wicks led the way. Everyone went running toward the clearing near the woods, with Winnie's dogs all yapping and howling underfoot.

"Over this way," said Wicks excitedly. He gestured

them toward an overgrown patch of brambles. Barney recognized it immediately as the spot he'd become entangled in the night before. A patch of his flannel robe was still clinging to the briars. "Here it is," Wicks shouted, "just like I told you. In all my years of hunting, I've never seen a print like this one. What do you make of it, Professor?"

Professor Baxter knelt down to examine the imprint in the muddy earth. "It's extremely large," he noted. He adjusted his glasses. "And it's most unusual."

"Is it a wolf print?" Cassie asked.

"It's definitely wolflike," the professor explained. "See the imprint of these claws? They suggest a *Canis lupus pambasileus* : your typical medium-sized timber wolf. And yet the configuration of the footpads would indicate a creature of far greater size and a different origin." He examined the print more closely. "Amazing," he gasped. "It's preposterous, but all indications would suggest *Neo-anthropus insipiens damnatus!*"

"What's that?" Barney asked.

"Some would say it's the most formidable of all beasts of prey," the professor replied. "It's *modern man.*"

Winnie moved closer. "What nonsense!" She raised her foot to trample the imprint into the ground.

Barney nudged Cassie. "I think Winnie is trying to destroy the evidence," he whispered.

Professor Baxter quickly pushed Winnie aside. "Don't touch that," he ordered. "You mustn't tamper with science. This print may have immeasurable research

70

value. None of my biological studies has ever unearthed such a specimen before."

"What does it mean?" asked Fred Wicks.

"It's too soon to tell. Perhaps the remoteness of these woods has produced a strange mutation unknown elsewhere." Professor Baxter quickly covered the print with his jacket. "I'll make a cast and take it to the university. Fred, go to my cabin and bring my equipment while I stand guard here."

"Sure thing," Fred said. "I know that thing was something weird the minute I seen it. *Unnatural*, that's what." Fred ran toward the lake to bring the professor back his equipment.

Horace Baxter seemed amazed by the discovery. "If this is what I imagine, it will add an entire new chapter to biology. If only we could trap such a creature."

Winnie was getting upset. "Nothing gets trapped on my land," she warned. "*Nothing*. Won't any of you ever learn? Why can't you take a lesson from the Indians? They tell us the wolf is our *brother*." Her face burned red with rage. "Things never change out here, do they? You slaughter the wolves, cut them open, and examine their remains. But you refuse to respect them and leave them alone. Leave us *all* alone!"

Aunt Alex placed her arm around Winnie. "Don't upset yourself, dear. Let's go back to the house."

"It's too utterly fantastic," Cassie protested. "The whole thing is a silly mistake or an awful nightmare or something. That can't be a werewolf footprint out there. Werewolves don't exist."

She and Barney were seated on the porch after lunch, staring out into the woods. It had been a miserable lunch. Winnie had been sullen and irritable throughout, furious because Professor Baxter hadn't joined them as planned. Instead, Baxter had packed up his plaster cast and driven it into Minneapolis.

"They *don't* exist—do they?" Cassie insisted.

"What doesn't?" Barney asked.

"*Werewolves*, of course. They're not real, are they?"

Barney didn't answer.

Cassie poked him with her boot. "Well, *are* they, Prescott?"

"How should I know? I'm no expert." Barney was about to refer to his library book when Crenshaw appeared on the porch. "Speaking of experts, what do you think, Crenshaw? What do you suppose that footprint is in the woods? Could it be human?"

"It didn't look human," Crenshaw said.

"Then it has to be an animal's print," Cassie concluded.

"It didn't seem to be from an animal, either," Crenshaw replied.

Barney stared at him. "If it isn't human and it isn't animal, do you think it could be a *versipellis*?"

Crenshaw stared back, then began to laugh. "You can't be serious! A *versipellis*? That word means a human who can change himself into an animal. *Versipellis* is an age-old *legend*, that's all."

72

"Are you absolutely sure?" Barney asked.

"Well, I'll admit many countries have shared similar folklore," Crenshaw said. "In Africa they've got were-hyenas and wereleopards. In South America they've supposedly got werejaguars. And in Japan there are werefoxes. Of course, in this country we've always stuck with the good old-fashioned werewolf."

"What if it's not just legend?" Barney asked. "What if werewolves are *real*?"

Crenshaw scratched his head in disbelief. "*Real*? All right, stop pulling my leg."

"I'm serious," Barney said. "Has anyone ever been accused of being a werewolf?"

"Certainly," Crenshaw explained. "Thousands of people have been accused of such shape-shifting. During the Middle Ages most of them were burned at the stake."

"Then werewolves were real once?" Cassie asked. "If they were real long ago, they could still be real now."

"If they had been real, they could be," Crenshaw conceded. "But if they weren't, then they aren't. That's basic logic."

Cassie was getting impatient. "You're supposed to *know* everything, so are werewolves real or not?"

Crenshaw grew thoughtful. "The question is more complex than I'd supposed," he admitted. "Literally speaking, I'd have to say yes: There *were* wild animal-men at one time. During the ninth century, a wild Teutonic cult known as the berserkers would dress up in the skins of wolves. By the full moon they'd ravage the countryside, doing dreadful deeds. They'd smash skulls and drink the blood of travelers. In fact, our word berserk is derived from their wild carryings on. Therefore, in one context, you could say werewolves were real. But on the other hand, modern psychiatry teaches us that wolf-madness is a psychosis known as lycanthropy. A person can actually believe himself transformed into a wolf and that person might behave exactly like a beast. But that doesn't mean he actually is a beast."

Cassie was disgusted. "Some big expert! *You* don't know the answer, either!"

Crenshaw hated having his knowledge questioned. "What brought up this ridiculous subject?"

"That footprint in the woods," Barney said.

"There's probably some sensible anthropological explanation for that print," Crenshaw reassured them.

"It isn't only the print," Barney said. "We met a man in town today who said he'd *seen* a werewolf out there in the woods."

"Was he a paranoid psychotic?" Crenshaw asked.

"He was a French-Canadian," Cassie said. "And he was terribly frightened."

Crenshaw stared out toward the woods where the late afternoon sun was casting a burnished glow across the trees. "Out there in the woods? This man said he actually saw a werewolf out there?"

"That's right," Barney said. "He called it a loup-garou, but that's the same thing."

Crenshaw got up and brushed some fallen leaves from his trousers. "I think I'll have another look at that footprint," he said. Then he walked hurriedly toward the woods.

Barney watched him go. "I'll bet Crenshaw is beginning to figure things out, too. That *must* be a werewolf's footprint out there."

Cassie shrugged. "It still seems crazy, but maybe you're right. With so many wolves prowling in the woods, maybe one of them *is* a werewolf."

Barney looked somber. "I don't think the werewolf is out *there*, Cassie. I'm afraid it may be inside the house—with us. In fact, I've an awful feeling the werewolf might actually be *Winnie Comstock!*"

Chapter Eleven

DINNER WAS TENSE THAT NIGHT. WITH THE COMING OF darkness Winnie became more nervous and irritable.

Barney mushed his mashed potatoes around his plate. "I think Winnie is acting paranoid," he told Cassie. "She's just like one of those nut cases Crenshaw told us about."

Cassie agreed. "She's definitely *berserk*."

From the other end of the table, Winnie glared at the children. "I told you I hate whispering. It's very rude."

Aunt Alex nodded. "Yes. If you children have something to say, share it with all of us."

"It's nothing," Barney explained. "We were wondering if Crenshaw examined the footprint in the woods."

"I'm afraid I couldn't," Crenshaw said. "Someone had tampered with it and it was gone. We won't know what it is until Professor Baxter returns."

"*I* know what it is," Winnie said. "It's nonsense. If Baxter thinks some bizarre life form lives in my woods, he's an idiot!"

Aunt Alex cleared the table. "You know what scientists are like, dear. They're always trying to discover something. Why don't we relax over a nice game of chess?"

"Not tonight," Winnie said. "There's a full moon tonight and I plan to take the dogs for a long walk in the woods."

Barney cringed. "In the woods? Tonight? Don't wolves *hunt* during moonlight?"

"I'm sure wolves see better in moonlight, just as we do," Aunt Alex said. "There's nothing strange about that, is there, Winnie?"

Winnie didn't answer. Her ears were tuned to another sound, far off in the distance, which only she seemed to hear.

"I'm going for a walk myself tonight," Crenshaw said.

"I'm not," said Aunt Alex. "Stumbling around in the woods isn't my cup of tea. I'm sticking by the fire with my knitting."

Barney didn't think it safe for Crenshaw to venture out at night. "Why don't you knit by the fire, too, Crenshaw? A walk tonight may not be too healthy."

"Don't be silly," Aunt Alex said. "There are no wild animals waiting to attack us. I'm sure Professor Baxter was right: The most formidable beast of prey in these woods is the *human*."

That's precisely what Barney was worried about!

Outside, the wind howled dismally, blowing the leaves from the trees and hurling them against the windows.

In Barney's bedroom, Cassie sat in the easy chair as she listened to him read aloud. "The original werewolf is the nightwind, the wild ancestor of the death-dog."

"Cut it out," she said, "that book is giving me the creeps."

"It's stuff we'll need to know," Barney argued. Fascinated, he leafed through the pages. "There's lots of stories here about ordinary people turning into werewolves. Some were perfectly normal until it happened. Some resisted by trying to protect themselves from the beast inside them."

Cassie stared at the barred window. "Do you think that's why Winnie installed those bars?"

"Maybe." Barney felt both repelled and obsessed by the information he was reading. "It says werewolf fits can affect a person every seven years. When it happens, the victim is doomed to spend time in wolf form."

"Do you think that's why Winnie moved out here seven years ago?"

Barney nodded. "She said she couldn't be around people. No wonder!"

The gruesome facts were quickly piling up against Winnie. "I'm glad she's not in the house tonight,"

Cassie said. "If she really is a werewolf, how do you suppose it happened?"

"She must've been bitten by another werewolf. That's the only way it can happen."

"There should be some way to recognize one," Cassie said helplessly.

Barney perused the book. "You can recognize them after they've been on the prowl," he explained. "Their bodies are all scratched up and they have a wild look in their eyes."

Outside, the dark hung heavy now. The moon was lower, sinking behind the towering cedar trees that could be glimpsed from the barred window. The sound of distant barking suddenly floated over the evening winds.

Barney froze a moment. "It's only the dogs," he said. He glanced toward the window, grateful for the thick iron bars. "It's brave of Crenshaw to go walking tonight. If Winnie is on the prowl, he could be in big trouble."

Cassie rose from the chair and nervously paced the room. "This is a nightmare and I refuse to believe it! We have no proof of anything, only circumstantial evidence. You can't convict a person on that." Technically, Cassie knew that wasn't true. *She* had been convicted on circumstantial evidence. When Mme. Fresnay had found the cigarette lighter under her mattress (where Victoria Wembly had placed it), Cassie was quickly accused of the dormitory fire. "Well, at least we *shouldn't* convict her on that evidence alone," she added.

"True," Barney agreed, "but the evidence keeps piling up—Winnie's long nails, her howling, the blood and claw on the carpet, the slaughtered dog—and don't forget that footprint in the woods. Remember when Winnie read us that poem she wrote? She practically admitted she could become a wolf."

"But we haven't actually seen her become a were-wolf," Cassie argued. "And seeing is believing. Face it, Prescott, you're a bookworm. You love reading weird facts, but it's still only legend and superstition."

"Maybe so," Barney said, "and maybe not."

As Cassie threw herself back into the chair, she heard the sound of the dogs barking in the distance. "Well, *I'm* not worried," she insisted. But secretly she felt helpless. Without money, Cassie *always* felt helpless. She could have kicked herself for spending her entire allowance. She'd left no money with which to escape. If only she had saved a few dollars. If only . . .

Cassie was so deep in thought, she didn't notice that eyes were peering at her through the window. The eyes had a strange, menacing purpose. They glowed steadily out of the background of pitch blackness. They were human eyes. At first Cassie didn't see the figure press its face against the pane or raise itself against the window to reveal the lean gray hairy shape of a beast.

From inside the room the lamplight cast a glow across the window. As faint gleams of moonlight glistened in the beast's eyes, Cassie finally glimpsed the creature behind the iron bars. It looked far more terrifying than any beast of prey for it was half beast, half human. Fur covered its back and partially concealed its face. Yet there was something strangely familiar about its features, part wolf, part man.

For a moment Cassie was filled with terror, paralyzed and speechless. As she stared at the horrifying sight no sound would come to her lips, no scream could be called forth.

She watched the creature lift its human hands toward the glass, scratching at the pane with its nails. Cassie finally rose from the chair. In a feeble whisper, she gasped, "Barney—look—there—at the window." Her voice faded away as Barney looked up from his book.

"Look at that!" Barney shouted. Jumping from the bed, he hurried toward the window just as the beastly figure turned and ran off into the darkness.

"Did you see it?" Cassie asked, her heart pounding.

"Sure I saw it. It was a *werewolf*. Like you said, seeing is believing. What a scary sight!"

"But that thing at the window wasn't Winnie," Cassie protested. "It was a *man*."

Barney scratched his head. "You're right."

"Well, what's it mean?"

"Nothing good, I'm afraid. It must mean there's more than one werewolf prowling around here. The beast we just saw is either the werewolf who originally bit Winnie or someone Winnie bit and turned into a werewolf."

Cassie groaned. "This is too confusing. One werewolf is bad enough, but two is too many! How will we find out who the other werewolf actually is?"

"I guess we can't," said Barney. "I guess it could be *anyone*."

Cassie threw up her hands in defeat. "So what'll we do now?"

"I suppose we'll have to tell Crenshaw everything," Barney suggested. "We'll let *him* tell Aunt Alex what's going on. If *we* tell her, she won't believe a word of it, anyway."

Cassie agreed. "You're right. Only Crenshaw could make all this sound sensible. He'll explain about the berserkers and the paranoids, and Aunt Alex will have to believe him."

As Cassie and Barney discussed this further, they heard the sound of the front door opening.

"That's probably Crenshaw back from his walk," Cassie said.

"Or maybe it's Winnie back from her prowl," Barney said. "We better be sure."

Cautiously they opened the bedroom door. Slowly they walked out into the hall, then tiptoed along the corridor that led to the living room.

They peeked in the doorway and observed Crenshaw pacing about the room.

"What's wrong with him?" Cassie whispered. "He looks really weird."

Crenshaw didn't seem to be himself. His clothes were torn in several places. There were scratches covering his face and a bloody bite on his arm. There was also a wild, frenzied look in his eyes. Cassie and Barney watched Crenshaw throw himself on the sofa, where he began to moan.

Barney quickly pulled Cassie away from the door. "Let's not speak to him tonight."

"Why not? We need his help."

"I don't think he can help us," Barney explained. "Did you notice that bite on his arm? I think it's the bite of a werewolf."

Cassie gasped. "Do you think *Winnie* bit him?"

Barney nodded. "And you know what that means, don't you?"

Cassie gulped. "I suppose it means that *Crenshaw* is the beast that appeared at the window! Now *he's* a werewolf, too!"

Chapter Twelve

"HOW CAN YOU SAY IT'S *OUR* FAULT?" CASSIE ASKED.

"Because it is," Barney said. "Crenshaw probably went out tonight trying to protect us because we told him about the loup-garou."

"*You* told him."

"Okay, *I* did. That's probably why he followed Winnie into the woods and got bitten."

"That's Winnie's fault, not ours," Cassie argued.

"But we can't let Crenshaw go around biting people, too! *We'll* be his first victims. Werewolves always attack kids first if they can. Kids are the easiest targets!"

Cassie still found it all hard to believe. "Crenshaw didn't look at all like the hairy beast I saw at the window. Out in the living room, he wasn't hairy at all."

"Werewolves don't stay hairy long," Barney explained. "When the fit is over they return to normal."

"I wish you'd never read that dreadful book," Cassie whined. "Now we've no one to tell and no one to help us."

"We could go into town for help."

"*Très* amusing, Prescott. Everyone in town is petrified. They'd never come out here."

Barney ran to the bed and picked up the book. "Maybe there's a cure." He flipped the pages. "Here's one. In certain cases some victims can be cured by drawing three drops of their blood."

At the mention of blood, Cassie's stomach turned over. All the dreadful implications of the evening suddenly hit her. "This is horrible," she moaned. "It's the worst thing that ever happened to me, the *worst*. I'd much rather be back with awful Madame Fresnay any day!"

During breakfast, Cassie and Barney stared at Crenshaw. They were amazed to see he looked almost normal. Nothing had changed except for the bandage he was wearing wrapped around his arm.

"What happened to you?" Aunt Alex asked.

"When I was out walking last night I got caught in the brambles," Crenshaw explained. "The next thing I knew, something reached out and bit me on the arm."

"What was it?" Aunt Alex asked.

Winnie looked embarrassed. "I'm afraid it must've been one of my dogs. Sometimes they get frightened when they hear footsteps in the woods."

"Poor Ollie," said Aunt Alex sympathetically. "You have scratches all over your face, too."

"Indeed I do," he replied. "Those briars are treacherous. All things considered, it was a most regrettable walk."

"You should have taken my advice and sat by the fire," Aunt Alex said. "That's what I did. Then I toddled off to bed and slept like a baby. *Nothing* could have woken me."

"I'm sorry I didn't do the same," Crenshaw said. "I feel positively dreadful this morning, not like myself at all." He pushed aside his uneaten breakfast.

Aunt Alex looked concerned. "What happened to your hearty appetite, Ollie? You're right, you're definitely not yourself."

"That's a fact," he agreed. He rubbed his bandaged arm. "I hope this bite doesn't become infected."

Cassie and Barney glanced at one another. They excused themselves and hurried into the living room.

"Did you hear what Crenshaw said?" Barney asked. "He admitted he didn't feel like himself. Werewolf blood must be running through all his veins by now!"

"Do you think he knows he's a werewolf?" Cassie asked.

"Maybe not yet, but after another full moon he's bound to find out. We'll have to draw some blood from him right away." Barney noticed Aunt Alex's sewing basket resting by the fireplace. He rummaged through it and found two long embroidery needles. "These ought to do the trick," he said. He handed one to Cassie. "You stick one in Crenshaw's chair and I'll put the other in Winnie's. Let's try curing both of them."

As Crenshaw entered the room, Cassie quickly placed the needle in the cushion of the easy chair in which he always sat.

Crenshaw glanced at her suspiciously. "What are you fussing with over there?"

"I'm just propping up your pillows," Cassie said innocently. "Sit down here and rest and you'll feel better."

Crenshaw approached the chair. "I'm glad you're finally learning some manners, young lady. A few months under my tutelage and you may actually become a likable person." Crenshaw proceeded to sit down. He had barely hit the cushion before he jumped up again. "Ouch! I've been stabbed!" He turned and stared down at the chair. The needle was clearly visible in the center of the cushion. He plucked it out and held it up toward Cassie accusingly. "I expect you are responsible for this childish prank?"

Cassie felt trapped. "It wasn't *my* idea," she protested, glancing toward Barney.

"Don't attempt to blame your cousin," Crenshaw said sternly. "I'm quite aware who the troublemaker is around here."

"It *wasn't* my idea," Cassie insisted.

Crenshaw's face grew red and his cheeks puffed out like a frog's. "Did you place this needle in my cushion, young lady?"

"Yes, but . . ."

"No buts," he replied hotly. "There are no extenuating circumstances for such behavior! I suggest one hour of extra study for you today." He stared down at the chair again. "Are there any other surprises awaiting me?"

"No, sir."

Crenshaw grabbed his book from the end table. "I don't think I'll take chances," he said, leaving the room.

Cassie glared at Barney. "Thanks a heap, Prescott!"

"Okay," Barney said as he and Cassie sat in the bedroom that afternoon, "I'll admit my needle therapy didn't work."

"It was a disaster," Cassie said. "You owe me a chunk of my life! Crenshaw made me do an extra hour of *math*, which is ten times worse than anything."

Barney handed her the book. "While you were studying I found another remedy," he explained. "This one will work for sure."

Cassie read down the page. "Are you crazy? We can't do this."

"Why not?"

"We'll have to cook up a pot of castor oil, tar, and vinegar, then pour it on the werewolf while we hit him with twigs. Crenshaw will never let us do that to him!"

There was a knock on Barney's door. He quickly hid the book underneath the bed as Aunt Alex entered.

"I'm taking you both out this evening," she explained. "Winnie says there's a Harvest Moon dance at the grange hall in town. I think you children will enjoy it."

"A harvest moon?" Barney asked nervously. "That's a *full* moon, isn't it?"

"That's right," Aunt Alex said.

"Will there be lots of people at the dance?" Cassie asked.

"That's right."

"Will Crenshaw come with us?" Barney asked.

"That's right, he'll be our chaperon."

Cassie and Barney both knew that a werewolf fit might strike Crenshaw during the full moon. They didn't want to be anywhere near him when it did.

"I'm not going," Cassie said. "I'm staying right here tonight."

"Don't be silly," Aunt Alex said. "I know Ollie gave you extra work today, but you mustn't hold a grudge."

"It's not a grudge, it's a cold. I'm catching a cold." Cassie pounded her chest and pretended a cough.

"I'm catching it, too," Barney said. "I'm not going, either."

Aunt Alex felt Cassie's forehead. "It's as cool as a cucumber." Then she felt Barney's forehead. "You both seem perfectly fine to me," she stated. "A change of scene will do you good. We'll leave at eight o'clock. Luckily I brought my high heels for the occasion." Aunt Alex blew them both a kiss, then closed the door.

Barney sighed. "What a mess. We can't let Crenshaw go into town tonight. What if he bites someone? He could start an *epidemic*. Pretty soon, everyone in Blue Ridge will be a werewolf!" He hurried toward the bed and grabbed the book from underneath. "We'll try this remedy right away. Before lunch let's mix up a batch of this glop."

Cassie glanced at the recipe. "It's hopeless. We'll need twigs from an ash tree. That's supposed to ward off evil beings."

"No problem," Barney said. "During our botany lesson Crenshaw pointed some out to me. There are lots of ash trees growing by the lake. C'mon, let's go."

During their walk to the lake, Barney had no problem collecting the tar needed for the spell. "We'll scrape the pine tar off these," he explained, gathering up fallen pine branches.

After gathering the pine needles and twigs from the ash tree, Cassie and Barney returned home. Luckily Winnie had a bottle of castor oil in the medicine cabinet and a jar of vinegar in the cupboard.

Cassie stood guard by the door while Barney boiled up the ingredients on the stove. "Hurry it up," she ordered, "it'll be lunchtime soon."

The recipe was complete and cooked before lunch. Cassie placed a lid on the pot, then Barney hid it under the kitchen sink.

There was a chant that went along with the cure:

> Graywolf ugly, graywolf old
> Do at once as you are told.
> Leave this man and fly away
> Where it's night and never day.

"I'm not reciting that silly thing," Cassie insisted. "There's a limit, Prescott."

Barney agreed. "Okay, let's mumble it to ourselves."

"This will never work," Cassie said. "We'll never be able to dump that glop on Crenshaw's head without him noticing."

A few minutes later Crenshaw entered the kitchen. "What is that unpleasant odor?"

"I don't smell anything," Barney said. "Do you smell something, Cassie?"

"Not a thing."

"Don't be foolish," said Crenshaw testily. "It's a dreadful odor fouling up the entire kitchen." Crenshaw sniffed around the room, then headed toward the cabinet beneath the sink. As he opened the door he noticed the pot resting on the shelf. "This is the culprit," he said, lifting the lid.

Barney quickly grabbed the ash twigs from the table. "Now's our chance," he whispered. "You swat him with these twigs while I shove his head into the pot."

Crenshaw bent over to sniff the contents of the pot. "What's in here, old army boots?" As he replaced the lid, Barney made a running jump toward him.

Before Crenshaw knew what had happened, Barney rammed into his back, then pushed his head toward the rim of the potful of stinky, sticky liquid. Meanwhile, Cassie swatted Crenshaw's rear end with the ash twigs.

Just then Aunt Alex came to the kitchen door and observed the bizarre sight. "What on earth are you children doing?"

Cassie quickly hid the twigs behind her and Barney backed away.

91

Barney tried thinking fast. "Cassie pushed me," he explained. "Then I bumped into Crenshaw and he fell into the—that stuff over there."

"What stuff?" Aunt Alex asked.

Crenshaw rose and caught his breath. "They tried to asphyxiate me!" he shouted.

Aunt Alex was stunned. *What?*

"Asphyxiate," he roared. "These children tried to suffocate me in that pot of swill!" Crenshaw's face grew berry-red. "I warned you, Alex. I advised you not to take these children under your wing. One rotten apple can spoil an entire barrel! Cassie has obviously gotten Barney to go along with her on her latest prank." He straightened his clothing and wiped his forehead. "I refuse to endure any more of this behavior. I promised to be loyal to the Ludlingtons, but this is beyond the call of duty!"

"I don't blame you for being upset," Aunt Alex said. "Still, there must be some explanation."

"Almost suffocated in swill!" Crenshaw repeated. "It's entirely too much to bear!"

Aunt Alex approached the pot and sniffed its contents. "What is this dreadful stuff?"

Cassie tried looking sick and helpless. "It's a cold remedy, I mixed it up myself. I told you I wasn't feeling well."

"A cold remedy?" Aunt Alex asked. "What's in it?"

"Just some herbs. They're used all the time in Switzerland." Cassie feigned a cough.

"We didn't know Crenshaw would fall into it," Barney said. Then he joined Cassie for a coughing attack.

92

Aunt Alex placed the lid on the pot. "I knew there was a reasonable explanation."

Crenshaw almost burst. "You don't actually believe that feeble story, do you? Alex, these kids are involved in something devious—*look* at them."

Aunt Alex looked at Barney and Cassie. "You're right, they look off-color. I should have listened when they said they weren't feeling well." She spied the bottle of castor oil resting on the counter where Barney had left it. "This will do the trick," she said. Taking two tablespoons from the drawer, she approached the children. "Open up real wide."

Cassie and Barney groaned. There was no way of avoiding their medicine without admitting their lie. Reluctantly they opened their mouths and swallowed the thick brown liquid.

"Now go to your rooms to rest," Aunt Alex ordered.

Crenshaw stared at the children as they hurried off. "I'll be keeping a close eye on you *both* from now on," he said sternly. "Nothing else will slip by me, so be on your guard!"

Chapter Thirteen

"I DON'T BELIEVE THIS MESS," CASSIE SAID. "NOW CRENSHAW will be on my case for life. Why didn't you *say* something in my defense?"

"What could I say?" Barney argued. "We can't tell the truth; the poor guy probably doesn't know he's a werewolf. But now I know what you mean about circumstantial evidence. It's not fair to convict a person on it."

At Aunt Alex's instructions, Cassie and Barney were seated on the porch, in the hopes the afternoon sunshine might improve their colds. Barney was curled up in the wicker lounge, watching the dogs scamper through the bushes. "At least we accomplished something," he said. "We won't be going out tonight. As long as Aunt Alex thinks we're sick, we can skip the Harvest Moon dance."

"It's time we told Aunt Alex everything," Cassie said. "Your stupid cures didn't work, so we'll have to tell her."

"First we'll need proof. That's not the kind of thing you tell a person without having proof."

"How will we get it?" Cassie asked.

"Maybe we can *trap* Crenshaw," Barney suggested. "Professor Baxter has lots of stuff in his cabin for trapping squirrels and things. We could use it to trap a werewolf. Maybe Fred Wicks has stuff we could use, too."

"Okay," Cassie said, "but let's do it before dark. I want to be indoors before the full moon comes out!"

Luckily Aunt Alex thought an "invigorating walk around the lake" would do wonders to dispel whatever germs the children were harboring. As Cassie and Barney walked toward the woods, the late afternoon sun was pouring its golden glow against the trees, dancing bits of copper light against the burnished leaves.

"I hope this trap idea works," Cassie said. "Which werewolf do you think will fall into it?"

"I hope it's Crenshaw," said Barney. "If we can trap Crenshaw while he's in wolf form, we might still save him from his dreadful fate."

"I hope so," Cassie said. "Who needs a werewolf as a tutor!"

"Whichever one we trap, at least we'll have proof of what's going on."

Cassie and Barney approached Professor Baxter's

cabin. They noticed the door was slightly open, the wind blowing it by the hinges. Horace Baxter had been so excited when he left for Minneapolis, he'd neglected to lock up.

"We're in luck," Barney said. He pushed the door open further and glanced around the cabin. Before his hasty retreat, Professor Baxter had been busy. An entirely new collection of dead things, their bones picked clean, was assembled on his laboratory table. Each group had been carefully cataloged with its Latin name written underneath.

Cassie stared into the eyeless skull of a raccoon. "Let's hurry and find the traps before I get the major creeps."

Barney rummaged around but found only a few dozen mousetraps. "We can't catch a werewolf with these!"

"Is that all he has, mousetraps?"

"I guess so," Barney said. "I forgot Baxter doesn't kill most of his specimens; he finds them dead already."

"We'd better check Fred Wicks's cabin," Cassie suggested.

"But we can't break in and we can't tell him why we need the trap. Wicks is a hunter. If he finds out Crenshaw is a you-know-what, he'll *shoot* him."

Cassie glanced through the cabin window. "It'll be dark soon, let's *hurry*."

When Cassie and Barney reached Fred Wicks's cabin they knocked, but no one answered. Barney glanced in the window and noticed several rifles neatly hung in their racks. "I guess he's gone to the big dance at the grange."

Cassie grew frightened. She knew nightfall would come soon, and the beast might be on the prowl again. "Maybe Fred has something stored on the porch," she suggested.

She and Barney rummaged through several crates that were stacked in the corner. Inside, they found dented canisters, raggy clothes, empty bottles, and food cans. "This must be his garbage," Cassie said.

The contents looked like trash, but at the bottom of one box, Barney discovered a large, rusty old metal trap. "Fred must've thrown this old thing out, so it'll be okay if we take it." He pulled the rusty apparatus from the crate and noticed it had a long length of steel chain attached to it. At the end hung a long hook.

"Do you think it'll still work?" Cassie asked.

"I can't say for sure until we try it," Barney said. "Let's hope so."

Cassie and Barney returned just as dusk was falling. They carried the trap to the side of the house and placed it underneath Barney's bedroom window. Then they dug a small hole, inserted the trap inside, and covered it with leaves.

"When a werewolf comes prowling, we'll be ready for it," Barney said.

After dinner, Cassie and Barney felt restless. They sat poised on their chairs like two vultures preparing to pounce. Their eyes darted around the room every time Crenshaw or Winnie got up. Were they about to leave? When would they transform themselves? When would they start to howl?

"What are you children *staring* at?" Winnie asked, more nervous than usual. "What's wrong with you two?"

Aunt Alex put down her knitting and glanced at the children. "Yes, they *are* acting strangely," she agreed. "Is it those cold germs? Perhaps they should go to bed. Maybe we should *all* make it an early night."

"No, Alex, you can't go to bed now," Winnie insisted. "Goodness, it's only seven o'clock. In fact, you could still make that party at the grange hall. Why don't you go? Farley hasn't left yet. He could drive you into town."

Aunt Alex was tempted. "I'd love to put on my dancing shoes. But I wouldn't like to leave the children while they're ill."

Crenshaw was seated by the fireplace, reading. As he looked up from his book his eyes seemed strangely dark and sinister. "I'll take care of the children tonight. After all, I promised to keep an eye on them, and I always keep my promises."

"Sure, Alex, go into town," Winnie said. "It'll do you good to get away."

Barney was growing very uneasy. Why were Crenshaw and Winnie trying to get rid of Aunt Alex? He knew why: *Children* were the easiest prey for werewolves! "No, you can't go," he pleaded. "Please don't go into town tonight, Aunt Alex. I don't want you to go."

"You don't? Why not?"

Barney knew the real reason sounded preposterous. Unable to think of anything logical, he blurted out, "Because you're much too old to square-dance. You'll make a fool of yourself."

Aunt Alex bristled. No one ever told her she was too *old* for anything. She threw down her knitting as if hurling down a gauntlet. "I'll have you know I can do-si-do with the best of them, young man! I think I'll call Farley right away." Then she hurried to her room to change her clothes.

Cassie threw Barney a filthy look. "Nice going," she snapped. "Now we're left alone all night with *two werewolves*!"

Chapter Fourteen

CASSIE'S HEART SANK AS SHE STOOD ON THE PORCH AND watched Aunt Alex drive off with Farley Hooper. "We should've told her *everything*," she said with regret.

Barney stared up at the sky. "The moon will be out soon," he said somberly.

"Should we try to make a run for it?" Cassie asked.

"Forget it; we don't stand a chance in the woods."

Crenshaw was standing in the doorway with a stern expression. "Come inside at once," he demanded.

Winnie stood at his side. "Yes, come inside and have some tea. It will help you get to sleep."

"No way," Barney whispered. "I'm not letting Winnie *drug* me."

Cassie agreed. "She's not sinking her claws into me, either. I'm locking myself in my room until morning."

Crenshaw's voice grew more insistent. "Come in at once; it's freezing out there."

Barney glanced toward the side of the house where he'd buried the trap. "Maybe we should stick together tonight," he suggested. "We won't get any sleep, anyway. We won't know if we caught anything until morning."

"You're right, we'll stick together."

Crenshaw's voice grew angry. "Come in or I'll come out and get you."

Cassie and Barney hurried into the house. The sky slowly became inky black, and the full moon emerged above the trees.

Cassie snuggled into the easy chair in Barney's room, buried under her comforter and piles of fashion magazines. Barney sat on the bed, reading a book. They both kept glancing toward the door to make sure it was safely latched.

An hour passed in heavy silence. No sounds were heard in the house.

Then suddenly, breaking through the stillness, the sound of the front door opening and closing alerted Cassie and Barney.

More silence.

After several minutes, the door opened and closed again.

"They've gone out," said Barney uneasily.

"Both of them?"

"Both of them."

"Do you think they've already changed into werewolves?" Cassie asked.

101

Barney shrugged. "I don't know. You suppose they have to go outdoors to do it?" He reached toward the night table for the library book.

"No, don't look it up," Cassie pleaded. "Let's not learn any more about werewolves; let's talk about something else."

"Like what?"

"I don't care. Tell me about your family."

Barney's family was a subject close to his heart, so he eagerly rattled on about them. But Cassie wasn't listening. She had suddenly become aware of a sound beyond Barney's voice. It was a sound from outside, very close to the house—the sound of footsteps crunching through the dried leaves beneath the window.

Cassie sat up. Was it a raccoon? Or a gopher or a deer? Or maybe it was all a nightmare. Yes, maybe everything that had happened was part of a super-realistic dream. Any minute Cassie would wake up and be back at Mme. Fresnay's Academy for Young Ladies. Any minute she would discover that Barney and Aunt Alex were figments of her imagination.

The sound outside continued. Cassie quickly fixed her eyes toward the window. There, by the light of the moon, a horrid beastly face emerged from the shadows.

Cassie closed her eyes, then reopened them. The beast was still there! Its claws were clutching the windowpane, its face was pressed against the glass.

As Cassie let out a piercing scream, Barney looked toward the window. An expression of terrified agony shot across the beastly creature's face and it let out an excruciating howl. Its clawlike hands slid down the glass, and its body suddenly disappeared from view as it slumped to the ground.

Barney ran to the window and looked out. "We caught it! It's stuck in the trap."

"*Who* did we catch?" Cassie asked. "Which were-wolf, Winnie or Crenshaw?"

"I don't know, we'll have to go see."

The unearthly howl of the trapped creature pierced the night air. "No, let's wait until morning," Cassie pleaded. "It's not safe to leave yet. If we do, the other werewolf might catch us."

The trapped beast howled again.

"We can't let it scream all night," Barney said. "First we'll get it free, then we'll tie it up."

Barney ran toward the door to unlatch it. As he did, the house was suddenly thrown into total darkness!

Chapter Fifteen

"WHAT HAPPENED TO THE LIGHTS?" CASSIE ASKED.

"They blew out," Barney said. "Let's get a lantern."

As Cassie and Barney fumbled through the hallway looking for a lantern, the beastly creature continued to howl outside.

Barney ran his hands across the empty hall table. "It's gone," he said desperately.

The beast outside howled again.

Barney stumbled toward the porch.

Cassie followed. "We shouldn't go out there," she cautioned.

"We have to." Barney pushed open the front door.

As they hurried outside, the howling suddenly stopped.

"Do you think the beast is dead?" Cassie asked.

"Maybe it *escaped*," Barney said.

"If it escaped, it will come looking for *us*. It knows we tried to trap it!"

Cassie felt a hand reach out of the darkness. It grasped her by the wrist.

"Where are you going?" a voice asked threateningly. It was Crenshaw.

Cassie tried pulling away but she couldn't. Crenshaw lit the lantern he carried and pointed it toward the children. "I told you I'd be watching you."

"You look *normal*," Barney said breathlessly. "Thank goodness you've changed back. We're sorry about the trap, but it was nothing personal. It was for your own good, honest."

"Please don't bite us!" Cassie pleaded. Beyond the flashlight's glow, another figure hurried toward the house. It was Winnie. Cassie gasped. "Oh, no. They're *both* going to get us!" She felt suddenly faint.

Winnie paused to catch her breath. "What's going on here? I heard strange sounds coming from the house, so I hurried back from my walk."

"I heard them, too," Crenshaw said. "It's another one of the children's pranks."

Suddenly, from the side of the house, the anguished moan was heard again.

Barney looked confused. "I don't understand. If you two beasts are here, then who's the beast over there?"

Crenshaw seemed equally confused. "Beasts?" he asked. "What do you mean? If you children didn't make that dreadful noise, who is responsible?"

"It's something that got caught," Barney explained. "We placed a trap under the window."

"A trap?" Winnie asked angrily. "On my land? Why?"

"We wanted to catch the beast," Cassie said.

Crenshaw scoffed. "What nonsense! What beast?"

There was no time for further explanations. Winnie's dogs were now awake and scratching at the screen door, begging to be allowed access to the trapped animal. Cassie and Barney no longer knew what or who they'd captured. Everyone ran around to the side of the house to investigate.

There, lying on the ground, was the werebeast. Its body was contorted, with its right foot caught in the trap's vise. Coarse gray fur hung down its back. But as the beast wriggled on the ground, it seemed to be shedding its wolflike appearance. The fur slowly fell from its back and forehead to reveal a human figure hidden underneath.

Barney was shocked to discover who it was. "It's Fred Wicks!" he exclaimed.

"A *third* werewolf?" Cassie asked.

"No, a *fraud*," Winnie shouted. She pointed at the wolf pelts that Wicks had used to camouflage his appearance. They had slipped off and were lying on the ground beside him.

"You mean there aren't any beasts around here?" Barney asked.

"I'm not so sure," Winnie said angrily. "Wicks has behaved quite beastly. He's been trying to scare me off

106

my land for a long time. I suspected what he might be up to, but now I have proof."

Fred Wicks's face was contorted in pain. "Get me out of this thing," he pleaded. He clutched his foot, which was caught inside the trap.

"Not so fast," said Winnie threateningly. "First you've got lots of explaining to do. Admit you're the one spreading those awful stories about me around town. You got the locals all fired up, didn't you? What did you tell them, that I was a madwoman? Is that why everyone is afraid of me? Is that why no one will come out here?"

"*Please,*" Wicks begged, "get my foot loose."

Winnie leaned over the hunter, vengeance in her eyes. "I should leave you there to rot. An eye for an eye, right, Wicks? I'll bet you've caught hundreds of wolves in traps like these."

Crenshaw knelt down to extricate Wicks from the trap. He released the vise from Wicks's foot. "I don't think there's too much damage. Your heavy boot protected you from major injury."

Fred rolled over on the ground, removed his boot, and massaged his injured foot. "Who put that trap there, anyways?"

"I did," Barney admitted. "Me and Cassie were scared. We saw you at the window last night and thought you were a real werewolf. So we decided to trap you."

"A *werewolf*?" Crenshaw asked. "I told you that was ridiculous."

"Well, we didn't believe you," Cassie said. "We believed our own eyes instead!"

"It all makes sense now," Winnie said. "Wicks wanted to scare the children, hoping they'd go into town and corroborate his wild stories about me. I knew he was up to something evil." Winnie stared at Wicks accusingly. "You'd stop at nothing to drag me off my land. But I warned you this would never be hunting land again, *never*. You're the one who killed my dog last night, aren't you? Then you made it look as if some beastly creature had slaughtered it."

"That was *your* dog the hunters found in the woods?" Barney asked.

Winnie nodded. "The poor thing was a stray I'd taken in. It wandered into the woods a few days ago and got lost. During my walk last night I discovered its body. I gave it a decent burial down by the lake."

"That's why we found blood on the carpet," Cassie said with relief. "We imagined something *awful*."

"Yes," Winnie said, "awful things have happened and Fred Wicks is to blame for all of them. I'm sure he planted that phony print in the woods for Baxter to find. You see, he wanted everyone to believe I was some kind of *monster*. He hoped the townspeople would be frightened enough to drive me off my land. Then he could buy up my property cheaply and kill off all the wildlife." Winnie stood over Fred Wicks menacingly. "Admit it, Wicks, you caused all this trouble."

"I don't admit anything," Wicks said. He tried to get up, but the pain in his foot made him fall back onto the ground. *"You're* the one in trouble, Winnie Comstock. You can't go around setting traps for decent people; that's *illegal.*"

"That isn't Winnie's trap," Cassie said. "We found it outside *your* cabin, Mr. Wicks. It's yours."

Winnie laughed triumphantly. "Very interesting. That will mean a twenty-thousand-dollar fine or a year in jail for you."

"I don't care," Wicks shouted. "I'd do it all over if I had the chance. Sure I wanted people to think you were a monster, because it's true. Nothing's the same since you moved out here." Anger rose in Fred Wicks's voice. "We don't want no wolf-lovers here, *nossir.* I used to be *somebody* back in the old days. When I came into town with my bounty, everyone would sit up and take notice. Why'd you have to come along and get the law changed? Why'd you have to spoil everything? Wolves are *devils,* I tell you. They destroy the game— game that belongs to us hunters. Okay, so I started those stories in town. It didn't take much to get people believing 'em, neither. That's 'cause no one wants you around here, Winnie Comstock, *no one.*"

The headlights of Farley's pickup could be seen coming up the road. When he had stopped the van, Farley noticed the confusion by the side of the house. He followed Aunt Alex over to investigate.

"Why are you children up at this hour?" Aunt Alex asked.

"What's wrong with Fred?" Farley asked.

"I want that man off my land," Winnie demanded.

"Farley, you're deputized; take Wicks into town and put him in the sheriff's custody."

"Why, what's he done?" Farley asked.

As Winnie held up the trap, Farley stared at it. "Hey, that's a Newhouse fourteen. I haven't seen one of those in years."

"That's because it's been outlawed," Winnie said, handing it over. She also handed Farley the two wolf pelts Wicks had used to camouflage himself. "Illegal trapping," Winnie explained. "That's the evidence. Now get him out of here. When you need me, I'll come into town to testify."

Farley helped Fred stand up, then led him toward the van. "Sorry, Wicks, but you've broken the law. The sheriff will have to handle this."

Fred slumped into Farley's pickup. "You haven't heard the last of me," he shouted, "not by a long shot!"

Chapter Sixteen

AUNT ALEX SIPPED HER COCOA BY LANTERN LIGHT. "WHAT went on here tonight? I don't understand one bit of it."

"I don't, either," Crenshaw admitted. "I was convinced the children had instigated all these childish pranks. I thought they rigged up that phony footprint in the woods, trying to tease us into believing it was a monster."

"We didn't instigate anything," Cassie protested. "We were trying to *help*."

"That's right," Barney said. "We tried to save your life, Crenshaw. We thought you had become a werewolf."

"You *what*?"

"Well, we did," Barney continued. "We thought a werewolf had bitten you. We hoped to cure you by taking your blood and by cooking up that potion you almost fell into."

Aunt Alex smiled. "Isn't that sweet, Ollie? The children wanted to help you even though they thought you'd turned into a beast. I'd say you behaved rather beastly, don't you agree?"

"No, I do not," Crenshaw insisted. "But if I have, it's because I know nothing about children. Caring for children is too big a responsibility for me, Alex. Are you sure you still want me as their tutor?"

"Certainly," Aunt Alex said. "We'd be lost without you, wouldn't we, children? Tell Crenshaw we'd be lost without him."

"*I* wouldn't," Cassie said.

Winnie poured more cocoa. "I'm to blame for all this confusion. I knew something suspicious was happening, but I didn't say anything."

Aunt Alex agreed. "Yes, you should have confided in us, Winnie."

"I wanted to tell you," Winnie admitted, "but I had no proof of anything. When my dog was killed, I couldn't prove Fred Wicks did it. Oh, I've been so nervous living out here alone. That's why I installed those iron bars for protection. Wicks has been sending me threatening notes for months, telling me to sell off and get out. Naturally he never signed them. I was afraid for my life. When you brought the children here I felt I couldn't endanger you all. I tried guarding the place and pretending nothing was wrong."

"I still think Fred Wicks must be an idiot," Aunt

Alex said. "How did he expect people to believe there was a monster loose in these woods? Anyone with common sense would know better."

Barney was insulted. "There was lots of circumstantial evidence."

"That's true, Alex," Crenshaw agreed. "Besides, it's common knowledge people believe whatever they choose. The townsfolk resented Winnie, so it was easy for them to believe the worst possible things about her. That's human nature."

Cassie glared at Crenshaw. "*You* believed the worst possible things about *me*, too," she said accusingly.

Crenshaw glared back at Cassie. He stifled an uncontrollable urge to stick his tongue out at her. "You believed the worst about *me* as well."

Aunt Alex sighed. "Yes, I understand how the children got carried away and jumped to conclusions. But folks in town must have mush between their ears. How could grown-up, mature people believe that Winnie is a werewolf? How could Fred come up with a wild idea like that?"

Barney gulped. "I guess he saw Winnie howling in the woods!"

Aunt Alex nearly choked. "What did you say, young man?"

Barney gulped again. It was out now, no taking it back. "It's true. We saw Winnie way out in the woods late at night, baying at the moon just like a wolf."

Winnie looked shocked. "You *saw* me? What were you doing way out there at night?"

Cassie didn't want Barney to reveal she'd tried to run away. "We were just walking," she said evasively. "We both saw you. You were howling."

Aunt Alex put down her cup. "Will someone let me in on the joke? Who's kidding who? Winnie, were you out in the woods howling?"

A strange expression crossed Winnie's face. "Yes, I was. That's my secret. I was afraid you wouldn't understand."

Crenshaw looked as shocked as anyone. "Is there some reason for such behavior?"

"There's only one reason," Barney said. "I'm afraid Winnie must be a you-know-what, after all!"

Aunt Alex grew impatient. "Winnie, explain what's going on."

Winnie was silent a moment. "No, I won't explain, I'll *show* you." She walked toward the window and glanced out. "The full moon is still bright. Come along, grab your coats. Follow me into the woods and discover my secret."

The moonlight on the lake was glistening like tarnished silver as the five figures merged into the shadows of the cedar boughs. Winnie led the group through the spruce trees beyond the ridge and into the denser woods adjoining the forest.

Aunt Alex had changed from her dancing shoes into her hiking boots and was trudging along the path at a vigorous pace. Cassie's pace slackened. She wasn't at all eager to discover Winnie's secret. She tugged at

Barney's jacket. "Where is she taking us?" she asked nervously.

Winnie gestured from up ahead. "Come along, you two. The wolves will have gathered by now; they're waiting."

"Waiting for *what*?" Cassie asked as she tripped over a fallen branch.

"Quiet," Winnie said. She paused near the clearing. "We'll have to attune ourselves to the woods by behaving as the wolves do." The trees were now shimmering in the full moon's light as Winnie glanced up toward the sky. "See that star?" she whispered, pointing to the southern end of the horizon. "The Pawnees call that the Wolf Star. It's the brightest one in that part of the sky."

Crenshaw stared heavenward. "Did we tramp out here in the dead of night to *stargaze*?"

"I'm sure Winnie wants to show us something else," Aunt Alex said.

"That's right," Winnie said, "and I hope you'll appreciate it. The trouble with most people is that they don't consider themselves part of the animal kingdom. In order to understand what I show you, you have to imagine yourself an animal, just as I do."

"I knew it," Barney mumbled, "she *is* a werewolf, after all."

"Don't be foolish," Crenshaw said.

"Let's turn back," Cassie pleaded.

"Listen and learn," Aunt Alex insisted.

"First we all have to form a circle," Winnie explained.

She gathered the group together and positioned them downwind of the trees. Then she gestured for silence. "Don't make a sound," she cautioned.

Cassie reluctantly held Barney's hand. "It's all clammy," she complained.

"So is yours," he grumbled.

"Be silent," Aunt Alex ordered.

"Let's get on with it," Crenshaw said.

"Now we're ready," Winnie said. She raised her head toward the moonlight. Then she opened her mouth and began to howl. The eerie sound floated over the trees for miles. The echo finally subsided when it reached its destination in the deeper woods beyond. Then Winnie howled again.

Crenshaw stared in amazement. "What on earth is she doing?"

"I have no idea," Aunt Alex admitted.

"Let's leave," Cassie repeated.

Presently, a full-throated sound came back in response and the howl was returned.

"I think something answered your call," Aunt Alex said excitedly. "Is it a wolf?"

Winnie nodded. "Yes, it's a wolf. I've named him Duke. He was once a lone wolf, but he joined a pack and he's always the first one to speak up."

"How fascinating," Crenshaw said. "Do you actually communicate with one another?"

"Naturally," Winnie said. "Listen." She let out another cry. This time it had a different pitch and a totally different answer came back in response. The howl was higher and more insistent.

Barney couldn't believe it. "You're talking to it like it was a person. You're talking to a *wolf*."

"Of course I am," Winnie said. "It's nothing new. Environmentalists come into the woods to do this all the time. Wolves love to communicate."

"Just like porpoises?" Barney asked.

"We're *all* part of the animal kingdom," Winnie reiterated. "Would anyone else like to try it?"

"I would," Aunt Alex said. "How is it done?"

"It's very easy," Winnie said. "Imagine what it feels like to be a wolf, then let it out in a big howl."

"That sounds like fun," Aunt Alex said.

Cassie and Barney stared in wonder as Aunt Alex let out a loud wail. Then she paused a moment, awaiting a response. Presently a small chorus of howls, whines, barks, and whimpers began to answer back.

Aunt Alex was delighted. "They're *singing*. Listen, children, the wolves are singing to us. There must be hundreds of them out there."

"It only sounds that way," Winnie explained. "There're no more than a dozen in this pack, but they can sound like an army."

Barney was fascinated. "Can I try it?" he asked. He opened his mouth and called forth the loudest howl he could manage. As he did, he imagined he was a wolf prowling through the woods in search of prey.

After a while, when the sound had traveled through the trees, Barney received an answer. But it wasn't the

117

wild, deep-throated response they had heard before. This time it was a high-pitched whine, followed by several yelps, squeaks, and quavers.

Winnie laughed delightedly. "The young ones are answering you, Barney. The pups must be out of their den."

"You mean those are *baby* wolves?" Cassie asked. She was amazed that somewhere in the dense woods were wild baby wolves *speaking* to them. Once she'd heard the wolf pups respond to the calls, Cassie wanted to join in. "Can I do it, too?" She raised her voice to emit a high-pitched cry. The sound danced through the still night air. After a while, a full-throated vibrant call floated back.

"That's Freya, a she-wolf," Winnie explained. "Those were her pups you heard."

Cassie trembled with emotion. A *mother* wolf had answered her call. Within that magical moment, Cassie felt her anger and resentment lift. In a strange, inexplicable way, she felt herself one with her surroundings. As the wolves moved deftly and silently through the woods, continuing their chorus of songs, Cassie felt she was an integral part of their landscape. The expansiveness within their cries, the exhilaration of their responses, was meant for *her* and she understood them. She felt a tingle run through her body, and she began to laugh. "They answered me! They really answered me."

"I'll have to get in on this, too," Crenshaw said. He

opened his mouth and let out a howl much louder than anyone else had done.

"Careful, Crenshaw," Winnie teased, "you'll scare the wolves away."

Crenshaw's noisy call was answered by an even louder one.

"That's Duke's voice again," Winnie explained. "I'll bet he's wondering what all this ruckus is about."

It didn't take long for Crenshaw to get into the swing of things. He howled again. Then, in unison, they all lifted their voices in a chorus of howls. Presently the calls were answered by a deafening medley of hoots, shrieks, brays, yelps, barks, and whimpers.

Barney listened carefully. He quickly learned to discern Duke's howl from within the pack. It was a long, low howl sung in defiance of all those who would dare conquer him. It was the majestic song of the lone wolf. *Know me for what I am*, it seemed to say, *not for what I'm supposed to be*.

After several minutes, the vocalization ceased and the wolves became silent. The assembly had abruptly broken up.

"What happened?" Barney asked. "Why did the wolves stop talking?"

"It's time for the males to go hunting," Winnie explained. "Now Freya will go back to the den with her pups."

Aunt Alex sighed. "What a shame; I was just getting into the swing of it."

"Can we come talk to the wolves again?" Barney asked.

"Sure you can," Winnie said. "But you can't just talk; you have to listen, too."

"Oh, I did," Barney said. "I think wolves have an awful lot to say."

"Then you've learned an awful lot," said Winnie, smiling.

The next night, Winnie took Cassie and Barney out to sing to the wolves again . . . and the night after that. Neither of them minded the dark or cold. They were both too engrossed in the exotic adventure. By the third night of howling, they could tell one pup's squeals from another's and had given them all names. Barney named the loudest one Loco.

At the end of the week, Aunt Alex had an announcement. With mixed emotions she explained it was time to return home to the Ludlington estate. "Everything is shipshape here now," she said. "The law will take care of Fred Wicks, so Winnie has no more problem."

Winnie sighed and nodded. "I'll miss you, old girl. I hope it isn't years until we see each other again."

"It won't be," Aunt Alex said. "I promise."

On the afternoon of their departure, Cassie was sullen. "I don't understand it," she said. "I didn't want to come here, but now I don't want to leave."

"I'll miss the wolves," Barney admitted, "especially

the baby ones. I can imagine what each one looks like."

/ "So can I," Cassie confessed. A part of her longed to stay close to Freya. At night when the moon hung low like a great fireball, Freya's howls would still echo through the trees, but Cassie wouldn't be there to reply. "But I guess I'll get over it," she added brusquely.

Winnie sensed the depth of Cassie's feelings. She patted her on the back. "Chin up, no sloppy good-byes."

Barney's voice quivered as he buried his face in Winnie's shirt. "Keep talking to Loco for me, will you?"

"Sure I will. Next time you come to visit, he'll be all grown up."

Barney fought back tears.

"Don't be such a wimp, Prescott," Cassie said, fighting back some tears herself.

Aunt Alex hugged Winnie for several minutes. "We'll all come back, I promise."

Farley Hooper drove by in his pickup, and Crenshaw stacked the suitcases inside. "I'm taking you all the way to Grand Rapids," he said proudly. "Once a year a fellow ought to see the big city."

As the dogs yelped by her feet, Winnie brushed some tears from her eyes and waved good-bye to everyone.

Cassie and Barney sat in silence as the van proceeded down the wooded path and Winnie's figure grew smaller in the distance.

Crenshaw leaned against the suitcases. "All things considered, our first trip together didn't go too badly.

Maybe we'll all get accustomed to one another after all."

Cassie groaned. "I doubt it."

Barney looked glum. "I think I'll always miss the wolves. Why did we have to leave, anyway?"

"Brighten up," Aunt Alex said. "This is only the beginning. We still have an entire year of fun and adventure ahead of us!"

Barney stared down the road, which seemed to lead nowhere. Nothing could be as exciting as the adventure they'd just completed, *nothing*.

Or could it?